THE ASHES OF THE BROTHEL

KATRYNA LALOCK

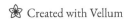 Created with Vellum

To those who'd rather burn bridges than ever have to look at them again

Prologue

IT WAS impossible to tell if I was surrounded by smoke or dust.

I knew that if I looked to the left I *should* have been able to see Cleopatra Hill. The hill was the focus of the last few years of my life; it was as much a part of me as this red dust clay that worked its way into my bones. That red dust clay was floating around me like a shroud now, threatening to choke me.

But I couldn't see old Cleopatra.

I knew that if I looked to the right I *should* have been able to see the valley that stretched below Jerome—named Verde Valley, because it was the only thing green on this goddam piece of land they called the Arizona territory. Clarkdale was somewhere down there, and in the other direction—where the mountains turned a vibrant rust so unlike any other color in my world—was Sedona. I knew this because I saw it every morning when I woke, but I couldn't see it now.

The smoke was piling up from that direction. The wind was doing nothing today to disperse it, allowing the smoke to wrap around my hair, press into my skin, water my eyes. It was messing my rag tag red hair from its smoldering bun. I raised my hand to it, wondering if it was still there, feeling singed bits that mirror my torn and melted dress. I paid a lot for that dress; women's clothing was a fine commodity these days. The population of Jerome was thousands on thousands but women? We were rare. We made up less than 20% of the population. This was going to be the devil to fix.

I jerked my head around as I heard someone cough to my left.

That couldn't be right, no one should have survived this fire. Certainly not me, but that's the beauty of last minute plans. Who would have imagined that I would be looking at the ruins of the brothel I helped raise to the top? Now it was a phoenix in waiting, ashes settled where buildings once stood, silence echoing through the unbreathable air. Would something come from it or would this finally be the end of this wicked town?

I wasn't going to stick around to see.

Chapter 1

I REMEMBER the first time I set eyes on Cleopatra Hill.

Pa, Ma, Heather, and I took the train to Arizona from Kansas. It was the first time Heather and I had ever seen a train, much less been on one. We lived in Kansas far from any real town, just a collection of cottages and a single grocer. Ma was sick at the time. Consumption racked our town and since Ma was a nurse, she got sick real fast. Most of our town was dead from it by the time we left.

"Head out west," Ma's boss, the doctor, told her. So Pa loaded us up in the train with what was left of our belongings. They had to sell a lot of stuff, Pa had to work a lot of jobs but, eventually, we got the money for the train. A wagon was out of the question. It would have cost almost three times as much and taken four times as long, so we rode the train until the day Ma died.

I hated Cleopatra Hill the minute I saw it. It was the back-drop for Ma's funeral as they burnt her body to nothing more than ashes. We couldn't afford a real grave since we'd just used all our money to travel out west, so the rest of the money that should have taken us to California got used up then. We stayed the night in Clarkdale and said our goodbyes to Ma. Heather cried for days. Pa didn't shed a tear.

The next day, Pa went around town looking for work when he heard of the mines just up Cleopatra Hill in Jerome. It was a day's ride by wagon and a bustling town. The year was 1895 and I was 17 years old. Heather was 14, Pa wasn't that old, but he just looked older in the days after Ma died. My parents had that rare love that my peer's parents didn't have back in Kansas. They supported each other, they loved each other, and Pa had every intention of bringing her to the ocean for her last few years. Instead, she spent the last of her days in a cramped train using a dirty latrine because we couldn't afford the normal carriage. I saw the fancy carriage through the planks in the train and watched the well-dressed children size us up with laughter in their eyes.

To say I hated my parents for uprooting my life would be an understatement. Ma always told me that women are the rock of the family and we have to let our men take some chips off us every so often: Flint to start a fire, pieces to secure the foundation. I'd rather a man never touch me with anything, much less anything sharp enough to take a piece off me. For her, though, I would be a rock. I was silent and sullen and still as the plains of Kansas gave way to the disgusting brown dirt of the desert.

"Can we see the Grand Canyon?" asked Heather, hoisting a book up at Ma and Pa. She couldn't see how deathly ill Ma was. She couldn't see that she could barely speak without blood flecks soiling her dress and her lips. She couldn't speak, she could hardly breathe. Heather was oblivious and would crawl into Ma's lap and open her picture book some family member gave her about the west. The book was mostly about California but it had a few pictures about Arizona territory and its Grand Canyon.

Heather thought we'd pass by, see it from the train. She'd always been foolish.

"Leave Ma alone," I scolded her. It's the last thing I ever said to Ma, or at least in front of Ma. She died the next day.

Consumption spread like wildfire through the cities exposed to it. It was custom to burn the bodies of the infected. Ma told me it would happen when she died, even if she recovered. She said you could never be too careful about consumption and the spread of illness. She warned me to always wash my hands when I could, always to keep clean, and to never breathe the same air as a sick person. Her getting sick anyway made her advice seem useless; yet Heather, Pa and I never got sick. It was a miracle.

And it was a damn impossibility to keep her from being discovered on the train ride over here with her condition. "Allergies," we had explained with a strained smile. She was a nurse, after all, why wouldn't they believe her? Consumption hadn't quite reached the west in the same numbers it did back home. No one thought to question us on the matter, even when others on the train got sick toward the end of the journey. When they saw Ma dead with all that blood on her mouth, they knew and kicked us right off the train, body and all. I still had nightmares of her slumped and lifeless body, tossed off the train with disgust so plain and open like I'd never seen before. I remember the wet thud she made when she hit the ground and rolled, leaving a trail of blood from her mouth. Even the church folk in the town of Jerome didn't look at the night workers with such venom. It was clear that we were scum of the earth.

"She got it trying to help!" Heather yelled at the train as the worker shut the door with a loud bang, stranding us a mere two hundred miles from the end of our journey. I was surprised they even slowed down to roll her out.

"She was trying to help!" Heather repeated, tears streaming down her tiny face as she ran after the train. Clarkdale, Arizona was where our journey ended. Ma never made it to the beautiful ocean she spoke so fondly of the entire train ride. She'd seen it once as a child and was ready to return to those sandy shores of San Diego or Santa Monica. Ma's body barely made it ten feet into Clarkdale, either, before the screaming started.

Pa picked Ma up like she weighed nothing (she really didn't weigh much, the consumption moved slow and sure and didn't stop until there was nothing left to take) and slung her over his shoulder and marched into town. Heather and I followed, dragging our meager belongings with us. Of course, we couldn't carry everything, so Ma's stuff was left behind. It took less than ten seconds before it was ransacked and gone forever.

We had nothing left of her, then or now. And when the flames finished and became embers, Pa scooped them into a jar and swore up and down that we'd give her a proper burial someday. He separated and saved the smallest bit of her in a jar he kept in his pocket. He didn't think we'd notice, but I saw. Heather probably did too, but she was so young...did she really understand? She knew enough that Ma shouldn't have been burnt like that and cried the entire funeral for her burned mother and dead mother, two separate offenses. Why did the world take her and then discard her so unceremoniously? A woman made of that much rock shouldn't be so flammable.

At least the train ride was manageable; the wagon ride was abysmal. There's no real bumps or hills in the part of Kansas we came from. Everything was flat and smooth farm land as far as you could see. Pa and Ma didn't have a farm. Pa was a carpenter and made houses for the township, but he could also build the most amazing furniture he'd always sell to those passing through. His hands were always rough but clean. Ma was a nurse. We didn't need a farm. We had neighbors who paid us for our services in foods and goods. Heather could sew better than anyone else and I was talented with math. We were still considered children then and allowed to be.

Our Kansas wagons didn't bump around like this one did. Every lurch threatened to unroot my teeth and upset my breakfast, which was some strange mixture made by a Mexican cook at our hotel. That was another strange thing about this place: I'd never seen a Mexican before. I'd never had their spicy food that made my stomach roll in ways I'd never experienced. Another lady that morning was so fascinated by my hair, I thought she'd cut some of it off for herself. I was used to the attention; it's rare to see something as red as my hair. And my freckles? I had more than the sky had stars. Just like Ma. This lady traced the constellations on my face with awe, mumbling under her breath in her foreign tongue.

My face was now as red as my hair from the brief moments in the sun for Ma's funeral, inflamed and itchy. A man sat next to me in the wagon, too close for comfort, with skin as pale as my own peeking from beneath his shirt sleeve. He reached into his pocket and handed me a small, unmarked bottle. "Aloe," he said, nodding vigorously. "You best find a plant, or make your own garden." I didn't take the bottle from him, so he shook it at me. "You dumb, girl? For your skin." He slapped it into my lap and went back to staring at the man sitting across from him, a scowl on his face.

The last lurching of the wagon brought us to the crest in Cleopatra Hill that signaled the start of the town of Jerome.

It was larger than any other place I'd ever seen in my life. The streets were alive and bright with wagons and people— mostly men—populating a strip of street filled with business after business. It took far too long for me to soak up my first sight of Main Street, which would become an intimate part of my life as I grew older. Pa put a hand on my shoulder and his other in Heather's and lead us down the dusty street toward the boarding house we were to be staying at until a more acceptable place could be found for a man and his two young daughters.

Chapter 2

BOYD'S BOARDING HOUSE was three stories (I'd never seen anything over two stories in my short life) and stood at the end of Hull Avenue, almost teetering off the slope of the hill. The porch barely clung to the dirt road as it wrapped around to head up the mountain, having run out of space to continue longways. The porch itself was made of threadbare planks with gaps wide enough to gaze down the mountain to certain death. They also rattled something awful when you walked across them. The house itself was on stilts above the wide open space below. It made it easy to dispose of trash and waste, but no one dared look out the windows at the back of the house. It'd give anyone a turn of their stomach.

Surprisingly, it was run solo by a woman who went by the moniker "Miss Kitty" and took in boarders after the death of her husband. It was all we could afford until Pa got a real paycheck.

We lived in a small two-bedroom box that was the size of our kitchen in Kansas. A fire the year before leveled most of the business district and took out many of the boarding houses.

Cleopatra Hill was so steep that well-built housing was hard to come by.

The other major problem with our living situation was that we shared our tiny box with two other men. See, rooms were rented by the shift in those days, so Pa's room was split between him and two other men. The mines were open all day, every day, with 8-12 hour work days. Whenever one man would be asleep, the other two would be at work. It went that way all day, every day, until Pa could afford to get us out of that place.

It wasn't too noticeable. Pa left once the sun went down and slept most of the day. Heather went off to school at the schoolhouse across town. I was too old for school, so I busied myself by exploring the town and finding odd things to do. Miss Kitty took pity on me and delegated me to tasks around the boarding house. I was much too old to be near the boarding house while idle and around the type of men that loitered there. I was lucky that most were dead tired by the end of their shift and didn't make unwanted advances. Only once or twice did a man actually lay a hand on me, but Miss Kitty was always lurking with her strict gaze to ward them off. After all, your landlady is the last person you'd think to cross, especially one as disagreeable to look at as Miss Kitty.

Those first months in Jerome were impossibly stale and undeniably boring. The work around the building was tedious but a welcome distraction from nothing. I had no friends, I was too old for the school house, and I had no skills to speak of. I knew a good deal of nursing from my mother and a mild amount of carpentry from my father, but neither of these tasks were needed. Miss Kitty tried to teach me the feminine traits I should have known; cooking, mending, sewing, working around the home.

She hoped I'd marry a miner. Little did she know.

My employment with her became short lived, ending about the same time Pa found the finances to move elsewhere. It was the week that Miss Kitty finally let me in the kitchen full time. Previously, I'd been set to sweeping, mopping and cleaning everything while the actual housekeeper, Gloria, flirted with the miners and snuck away with them. She was a hard eyed, cruel woman that would flog you for stepping out of line. Since my employment wasn't official, she felt that she could especially boss me around over those who were employed. After all, if I were too stupid to work elsewhere, I was too stupid for her to take kindly to. She made all sorts of mess for me to clean up and was particularly upset about my promotion to the kitchen.

Her favorite trick to play was to pour salt into my dishes when she thought I wasn't looking, then make a face as she tasted them. "No good, this one," she would say loudly to whoever was around. "No good, this dumb child. Stupider than piss." She would bellow a laugh afterwards, even when no one joined in. I was not particularly liked, but I wasn't disliked either. I kept to myself and did my chores on time and often helped others. No one dared stand up to her for fear of her rage, but no one exactly joined in on the fun either. I took that as a little boost of confidence.

One day, Gloria was feeling particularly callous. Her least favorite duty, all of our least favorite, involved cleaning the latrines. There was nothing fouler than a latrine used by a man. For the most part, they were just holes that opened down the side of the mountain but on the upper floors, they needed more maintenance. Chamber pots would be a generous way to describe them. She usually delegated the task of cleaning those to who were well below her.

That particular day, she decided it was my job.

"Louisa," she said, sliding up to me. Her small eyes that

were too close together narrowed on me with a ferocity I'd become too familiar with. "Louisa, you know you don't belong in the kitchen. Dumber than dirt, you are. Get up there and clean them chamber pots." I knew better than to argue, so I removed all the pots and pans from heating sources when she wasn't looking and made my way upstairs. If anyone wanted to complain about how long it took for supper, they could just look at Gloria—and I'd sell her for less.

The chamber pots were particularly atrocious that day. There was a rash of diarrhea going around, which happened every few weeks or so, and it looked like it was in peak that week. Thankfully, I had a strong stomach from working with Ma and her nursing patients all those years. I went about my duty without much complaint.

Gloria poked her head around the corner an hour later, an unkind smile on her face, "Dumber than the shit you're cleaning out, right Louisa?" I made no comment back, she'd regret her words before long.

Later that night when Gloria came around to do her usual taste test, I was ready. Before she came, I set aside a small pot and filled it with part of the chamber pot cleanings from earlier. I did little to mask the scent or its consistency. She looked at me with her usual venom, that hint of a smile at her own cleverness tugging at the edges of her lips. She slowly grabbed the salt and advanced on my dish. As she raised the salt over the pot, I said, without turning around, "I've already seasoned that dish. Go ahead and try it before you add more." She froze and I turned to face her full on, hands on hips, defiant. A rock that refused to chip. Her eyes narrowed and she picked up a spoon without even looking at the dish, lowered it to collect some of the liquid, then brought it up to her lips.

The minute the foul liquid passed her lips and went down

her throat, she gagged, bringing up the small amount she'd managed to swallow. In a sputtering cough, she looked down at the pot and her eyes widened.

"Is this shit!?" she screamed at me, her voice high and shrill. It was loud enough to make the others come running to see what the commotion was about. It didn't take too long for them to figure out what the hollering was for, and the other housekeepers had to cover their mouth to stifle their laughter.

"I must have mixed them up. You know, dumb as piss," I said with a shrug.

A day or two later, a miner died in that house. I wasn't allowed in the kitchen after that.

The remaining few days carried into tedium until Pa could afford an even smaller box, though one that didn't require public bathrooms or sharing rooms with random men, on the opposite end of town.

It just happened to be inches from the heart of Main Street.

Main Street broke off from Hull Avenue and skirted the mountain's edge in a way that was both thrilling and precarious. If Miss Kitty's place was nonsensical, then Main Street was downright stupid. It boasted a string of saloons, brothels, and restaurants so unlike the rest of town it was like walking into another world. Hull Avenue had churches; Main Street had whores. Pa put us under strict instruction not to go there—his main warning was for me. Heather was busy with school and her friends and their parents. She'd grown very close to a family down the road with too many children to count as it were. She was home even less than Pa and had no supervision to speak of.

Her hair often fell from its braids and flew about her face in an unladylike fashion.

Meanwhile, I put Miss Kitty's skills to work. The house was always clean, food was always ready. I did the shopping. I did the mending. Pa made furniture when he had the energy, which wasn't very often. We spent a few months sleeping on the floor of the strange, small house until he could fashion a bed for us all.

At least it was clean.

His warning to avoid the brothels was directed purely at me, probably out of fear I'd end up working there. Despite being in Jerome for almost six months, I hadn't made a single friend, had no job, and was at grave threat of falling into the precipice and becoming like the sex workers.

I couldn't deny that they fascinated me. I'd run into them more times than not; they were hard to miss. They dressed in the latest fashions modified to show more skin than was acceptable at the time. I saw them at the grocery and waltzing the street. Sometimes they would call to me as I walked down the street, exclaiming over the color of my hair. They loved to touch it and stroke it, a feeling that was alien and uncomfortable. I wore a bonnet from then on, despite how dated it was.

Still, I stole glimpses at their salaciously exposed skin. At night, I tried to peek into the windows of the brothel to get a glimpse of something, anything, but often was so terrified of getting caught I put as much distance between myself and them as possible.

I wasn't the only one who stared.

I headed down town one afternoon to settle a debt for Pa when I saw one of them up close. She was a full head taller than me and wearing the latest fashion in headwear. Her hair was the color of mud but it suited her and made her exotic instead of plain. The bits of her flesh that were exposed—bare ankles, sleeves that didn't completely extend to her wrists—were smooth and browned from the sun. She had expressive eyes the color of the malachite Pa brought home from the mines sometimes and her cheeks and lips were colored with rouge. She was the most beautiful thing I had ever seen.

She knew others were staring at her, which she responded to with a wink and a nod. She greeted most of the men that tripped over her by name and an occasional kiss on the cheek. No matter how grimy or disgusting they were, she paid them their bit of attention, as if they were the finest man she'd ever seen. It was the first time I met Rosemary Charm, a golden girl of Nora "Butters" Brown's Hotshop. She flipped open a fan to wave over herself despite the cool air of the October afternoon, which gave her a sense of drama and mystique.

That night, I labored over how to make my own fan. I needed to get another sight of it, to see the color, how it moved. My memory wasn't enough.

Hotshop was on the edges of Main Street in its own cluster of buildings. There were only six or seven "boarding houses for women" at the time and were either owned by Nora or Jennie, the two most infamous madams. They built their brothels at opposite ends of the street, two villages with plenty of buildings in between to declare clear boundaries.

Rosemary Charm worked Thursdays, Fridays, and Saturdays, that's all she needed to do. I followed the curve of the house to her room, finding the window partially open as it usually was this time of year. The air was cool at night but stuffy by day and she always cracked her window just enough to let the breeze in. The curtains were partially open from the wind that flitted through. I found my usual sitting rock and waited for her to bring a suitor in.

It wasn't long before I heard her tinkering laugh intermixed with the groan of the man she lead into her room. I straightened and pressed myself against the side of the house, edging along the precarious hillside behind it. It wasn't a long fall to the bottom but it would be painful and I'd be caught. I couldn't risk a disruption of my ritual.

I saw her bare back as she closed the door and locked it. She turned then to face him, to face me, and her entire beauty was exposed. Her breast were large and firm with light pink nipples that begged to be touched. The man obviously agreed with me, his hands reaching out to touch and caress her chest. She tilted her head back with a deep moan, her eyelids fluttering as he worked her. My own hands tugged at the buttons of my blouse, desperate to feel my own skin. My fingers slid over the now exposed flesh of my sternum, gently tweaking a nipple as I found it. I bit back my own moan.

Rosemary reached out to the man to undress him, a boring but necessary task. I watched the way her unbound hair swept across her shoulders, falling just below her breast, making them disappear momentarily. I was so transfixed, I almost missed the now naked man as he tried to pounce on her, but she held him back. She forced him back to the bed, giving me full sight of the scene.

I disliked this part—when she dropped to her knees and brought the man's penis into her mouth. It made my stomach roll to see it—the fleshy item disappearing between her full lips. Instead, I removed my hand from my blouse and gathered my skirts, dipping my fingers beneath them. I never wore undergarments on these nights, there was no need. I wanted access, I wanted to feel it all. I loved the way my slick wetness felt on my leg as I walked home afterwards, skin aglow.

Instead of his disgusting penis, her lips were my fingers,

tracing a slow line up my inner thigh, edging at the corners of my pussy. I could feel my heartbeat in those swollen outer lips, now slick with desire as I stared at her. I watched her red lipstick smear over his lower body and imagined her leaving trails of it up my thigh. Her fingers were digging into the meat of his leg, his hips, trying to keep him in place. My own hips bucked on their own accord as my fingers swirled over the sensitive bud at the peak of my slit. It always felt so strange but so pleasant, like I was doing something secretly wrong. At any minute someone could find me, a breast exposed from my unbuttoned blouse, hand disappeared under my skirts, riding my own hand.

It only added to my excitement.

Her eyes opened as she eased herself off his penis and I wanted so badly for her to see me. I wanted her eyes to catch mine through that open window as I'd imagined time and time again. I wanted her to see the lust and desire that matched hers. I wanted her to open that window all the way and invite me in.

Instead, her eyes trailed up his body to his face, her now empty mouth showing a wonton smile. The man was panting, his ugly face looking down at her with devotion and lust. It was disgusting to see her on her knees before someone as ugly as him. It was even more disgusting to see him reach out and lift her onto his lap, collapsing entirely onto her bed. He brought her down over his penis, burying himself to the hilt. She let out a cry, her fingers twisting over his shoulders, nails digging deep. He echoed her cry, though his was more of pleasure.

My angle wasn't good enough to see. I wanted to see the way her legs parted, the way she opened herself up for the men sometimes. Some liked to look and touch and lick and suck, I would imagine that was me. My own hand dove into my wetness then, burying a single finger as deep as I could at that angle. It didn't feel as good as circling my clit but it added something, a fullness I craved, a sensation I wanted more than needed. When I did it this way, fingers deep in my own pussy, one circling my clit, I came the hardest.

They were moving faster now and I knew he wasn't far from cumming. I was just behind so I closed my eyes, imagining that my fingers were hers, adding a second to myself. My thumb busied over my clit and I heard her gasp, heard her moan. My eyes flew open to see her head thrown back in ecstasy. How did she do it? How did she climax with just his sad, small, ugly penis inside her? And without any warm up, without his hands or mouth on her before?

I marveled at her, an absolute beauty in the heat of her ecstasy as I chased my own. The look of euphoria on her face drove me over, my thumb pressing hard on my clit as I felt the ripples of an orgasm. It came to a head then, burying me just before the man pumped his last few pumps into her.

I watched as she slid off, her body beautifully open to me then, her legs wide open to expose her soft pink flesh to me. I wished I was the one standing over her then, wished she was looking at me that way.

But here I was having to clean myself up, button my buttons, and head home.

Chapter 3

WINTER CAME in Jerome for the first time, and it was much different from winter in Kansas. I was used to the rolling winds, the rain, the snow, the sleet. Nothing like that happened in Jerome. It might have snowed once or twice over the sickeningly short winter, but for the most part, it was mild. Heather tore up our old winter jackets and coats and fashioned them into more summer and fall clothing. Despite being just 15 now, she was skilled enough to do this on her own, and took the time to teach me during her winter break from school. When she wasn't running around like a wild child with the neighbor's children, she was crafting like the handy seamstress she was. My work was passable, Heather's was phenomenal.

We continued our winter break in this way and I was glad to have a helper in the house. Pa even got a day off from the mines to celebrate Christmas and New Year.

Everything was going well.

Until the smelter caught fire.

The mines were underground and stretched for an eternity. Pa mentioned it once or twice while drawing its outline for

Heather. She ate up the architecture of the mine, fascinated by how it all worked. I was more concerned with the changes in Pa's eyesight from being underground all day and never seeing the sun, and how it affected his carpentry skills. His items weren't fetching nearly the price they did back in Kansas. Less time, less skill, and he was always so tired...

But the mine was underground, and for that reason, fires were a danger and would burn for months if they were not dealt with. Some parts of the mine were permanently closed off because the fires couldn't be controlled. The bosses knew better than to force men to work alongside the fires and the thick, cloying smoke. Pa already said most of their workers were immigrants from Mexico and China working for next to nothing a day. There'd been talk of creating groups to improve the quality of the mine work, even after the law of 8-hour work days passed.

Arizona was still a territory, and it was still lawless, and for that reason, the mines were never quite as safe as they should have been. One day, Pa went off to the mines just as the sun was setting, tipping his hat to us as he closed the door behind him. Heather and I went to bed, knowing that we'd be awoken in the morning by the sound of him in the kitchen. It was Sunday, the last Sunday of Heather's winter vacation before she returned to school. I would miss having her around but longed for my long days of solitude. I'd gotten used to doing so much work alone that her presence could be stifling at times. She was my sister, not my daughter, and it wasn't really my responsibility to raise her.

Morning came and Pa still hadn't come home. It wasn't entirely unusual for the workers to run over an hour here and there. Usually, though, Sundays followed a tight schedule on account of the Sabbath. Still, afternoon rolled around and there was still no sign of Pa. Heather and I dressed for the day and headed toward the mines in hopes of catching sight of Pa on his way home. The long walk to the mines were empty and met by no one. They were all at church, a place no one in my family could bring themselves to visit.

The streets remained empty as we headed down the hill until we got to the mine and saw the crowd of people gathered at the mouth of the latest tunnel.

Families stood together, holding each other and crying. There weren't a lot of families since most of the workers were immigrants and alone, but there were enough for me to understand something horrible happened. Heather knew too, she was 15, not stupid. She broke free from my grip and tore through the crowd to the mouth of the mine where Pa worked. Smoke billowed out from the opening and filled the sky above it with its noxious scent, the color of death. I stood transfixed, watching the smoke climb up the hill and obscure the sun directly overhead, making the winter sun nothing more than a hazy circle in the sky. Even on the coldest of days, you could always count on the sun to beat down on you endlessly. It reminded me of the last time I saw smoke like that—when they burned Ma's body before we could bury it.

But these plumes of smoke told an entirely different story as they curled from the mine. There were other deaths in this singed, scorched earth smell. It didn't belong to just one woman or one man. It was the funeral pyre to an entire company of men trapped under the earth in one of those tunnels Pa drew out crisscross across our table.

I don't know how long I stared at the smoke as it climbed into the air, or what snapped me from my reverie, but I saw Heather lunge for the open mouth of the mine. A woman grabbed her by the wrist with reflexes so quick they could only belong to a mother. Her face was tear streaked and ashen, but she held onto Heather with such fierce strength I didn't doubt she meant to stop Heather or rip her arm off trying. I caught up to her in time to yank my sister from the woman's grip and spin her around, looking her square in the face. "Don't you go off doin' something so stupid!" I hissed. I tried to keep my voice down for propriety, a funny thought now. I still didn't want people thinking we were savages. It was bad enough Heather ran around untamed as she did, and me unmarried at my age, still living with Pa. I knew the neighbors talked. In the chaos of the scene, no one would have noticed us in our poor, worn attire that was too thin to protect from the cold day. No one would have noticed us at all if Heather hadn't gone full tilt at the open mouth of the mine.

Heather collapsed onto the ground in a pile of nothing but clothes and childish fury. She lay there, unmoving, too consumed by her grief or shock or whatever else compels 15-year-old girls. I left her to find answers in the woman with the iron grip.

"You have to control that girl," the woman said. It was a strange sentence coming from a mouth that was gaping and sobbing. "You...you have to keep her in line," she insisted, grabbing my shoulders and shaking me. "Are you listening to me?" her voice grew in fever and pitch and I felt my brain rattle in my skull at her shaking.

A hand was placed gently on her shoulder from another crying woman. "Excuse Martha, her son and husband were in the mines." Her own tears were mostly dried, but she made the snuffling noises of suppressing more tears.

"What happened?" I asked after detaching myself from Martha's iron grip. As if I didn't know. Martha knelt to the ground then and buried her head in her hands, letting her sobs take over for her. Heather was still in her own pile just feet away, silently staring at the opening to the mine with her cheek pressed to the ground.

"A fire," the woman said, staring at me without blinking, as if it was the most obvious thing in the world. "A fire, in the mines," she repeated.

"Have they put it out yet?" I asked. A fire made sense, what with the smoke, but why hadn't anyone put it out? Didn't fires still have smoke long after they'd been put out? Ma's burning took quite some time. Bodies don't just burn if you light them on fire, you have to add gasoline or something else. An accelerant. And it takes a long, long time for the entire body to burn down. And even then the bones are left, and they have to be ground up into tiny pieces, otherwise you just have a skeleton. And if you miss the skeleton and just have the ashes, you're missing a huge part of someone.

"You can't put out mine fires," the woman said, her voice still strange and her eyes still wide and unblinking on me.

"Not even from the inside?" I asked, turning to look at the mouth of the mine again. Surely, they were in there, stomping out the fire. The woman said nothing and stepped back, leaving me to stand over my mute sister as she lay with her cheek in the dust, unmoving.

Neither of us noticed the passing of time, but we must have been there for a time because a man approached us and put a hand on my shoulder. "Miss?" he said hesitantly. "Miss? Who is you looking for?" He had a thick Mexican accent but spoke passable English. Pa said most of the workers in the mine didn't speak English except the other white men, so they had to find their own kind to speak to. Pa was picking up some words here and there and taught us them as we fell asleep at night.

"Pa...my Pa," I said, not understanding the question. "He

left last night and normally comes home by morning, but he wasn't home this morning." The man was silent and stole a look over my shoulder to someone I couldn't see and didn't bother to turn to look for.

"He in there, then," he said, nodding to the open mouth of the mine. "He in there and dead."

My head snapped up to look the man right in the face, eyebrows narrowed. "How in the hell do you know that?" I yelled at him. "Did you see his body? Did you go in there? Then you don't know. You don't."

Heather and I stood at the mouth of the mine until the sun went down that night. I bent down and touched Heather's shoulder. She roused only enough to let me lift her up, lifeless as a rag doll, and carry her a few feet. She was too heavy for me. Even with all the work I'd done around the house of transporting things, running errands, helping Pa...I wasn't strong enough to pick up a 15 year old girl. She fell from my arms and into the dirt. We were covered with dirt and soot from standing so close to the mine. Her face was red with the heat and bruised from laying in the dirt all day. "Heather, you need to get up," I said. She didn't respond. I shook her the way Martha did earlier that day, eye to eye with her. "Heather, get up. Get up! Get up!" I was screaming at her, over and over again, trying to get her to move.

She looked at me at long last, her brown eyes clear and certain as they looked right into mine. "Pa's dead," she told me. "We're alone. We're orphans." She spoke with such certainty, I didn't answer her for a long time.

"We don't know that," I replied. Something about the entire situation seemed surreal...just plain wrong. How did the fire even start? Why was it still smoking? Why did no one try to stop it? It didn't make any sense to me, not at all.

"Those fires burn forever," she told me. "I learnt it in school. The fires start and there's so much in the air down there they burn forever. They never go out. The original settlers set them fires to try to get rid of the white folk a few years ago and kilt a lot. Kilt them all, Louisa. Them fires burn forever and Pa is burning forever and we ain't gunna see him again." With this note of finality, she stood and put her small hands on my shoulder, looking me dead in the eye, "We're alone, just you and me. Until you die too and then it's just me." She dusted off her skirt and turned back to the house, not bothering to see if I was behind her or not. She walked with the surety that all children have in these situations. Heather accepted it. Pa was dead, Ma was dead, and we were alone in a strange town.

Chapter 4

NEEDLESS TO SAY, we couldn't afford that little box anymore. I dragged out our semblance of home as long as I could by selling what was left of Pa's pieces. They fetched less than optimal prices in what I could only attribute to my gender. I lacked the prestige of the socialized and civilized women of upper Jerome. They commanded attention and respect; I was just a child with soot smudged on her face and dirt under her fingernails. They took one look at me and knew I was an orphan and they could ring me out of everything, especially a fair price.

Eventually, everything was sold from the box and the reality of moving set in. While Heather was in school, I went looking for a place to work and a place to live, or hopefully, a place that would provide both. I knew better than to go back to Kitty Boyd's boarding house after what happened with the dead miner. No one blamed me for the trick on Gloria with the latrines, she had it coming. And while no one could prove I was the one who killed the miner, it looked mighty suspicious.

I saw him talking to Heather one of those last morning on

the porch. It seemed harmless enough. There weren't many children in the boarding houses. Most of the men didn't have the time or resources for a family. Still, others left their families behind, along with their children. They were always respectful of Heather and crass to me, which I understood. I was about the same age as the women on Main Street they frequented.

But this man was different. As the days went on, he was more and more involved in Heather, asking her to come to his room after hours. She confided in me one early morning that he scared her, and she was worried he might hurt her. It wasn't too much later in the week before he was found dead in his room, bleeding from every opening on his body.

It was suspicious and risky on my part. It would have been easier to do any other number of things to end his life, like pushed him off the edge of the hill while drunk. But I took the quick route, the easy route. I filled his supper with a box of rat bait. Part of me wanted him to die slowly, the other part knew that if it were too slow, he would live to tell everyone I gave him the food that ended his life. So I settled for the whole box of poison, thinking he was about the size of a box full of rats.

Pa, Heather, and I moved out within the week for unrelated reasons, and no one *formally* blamed me. But Miss Kitty stopped letting me in the kitchen from that moment on, and I knew I wouldn't be invited back if I asked. I also knew that the other boarding houses wouldn't be ideal because we'd run the risk of the same thing happening. Too many miners, too many grabby hands or long stares or "just come to my room later."

I settled, at long last, for working in a grocery and general store on Hull Ave. It was the second largest in Jerome and boasted exotic food from the homeland of the immigrants. It was also the prime place to come and get your clothes mended, which is how Heather helped out on days she didn't go to school. We lived in a room above the store with the store keeper and his family. The store was owned by one of the rich members of Jerome society who lived up on the hill in a real home. He was owner of half a dozen other buildings and businesses in Jerome, but believed fully that his staff should live in comfort. Part of owning the store meant the managers had a place to sleep and food to eat. They didn't work terrible hours and the staff was given holiday pay. The downside was that the store was open every hour of every day to accommodate the schedules of the miners. This meant that the housing above the shop was not particularly quiet. All times of the day, you could hear the ruckus below. Heather hated living there, but she understood how dire our circumstances were and never complained about additional work. I think she actually liked mending clothes on the weekends, especially since it was with all the older women of the shop.

My duties were varied and also included attending church with the store managers. They were staunchly religious and did not accept their employees straying from God. Heather was good about sitting through sermon and not causing a problem, I had much more trouble. I hated the hard, ridiculous seat and the long drawn out sermons. I'd rather spend that time sleeping, since I so rarely slept these days. Between worrying over money and my future and the loud streets below our home, I never slept more than a few hours at a time. I also had no hobbies to busy my free time and often found myself prone to panic if left idle too long.

Another part of the manager's staunch religious views included his aversion to all things involving the working women of Main Street. He would cross himself whenever they entered the building and speak to them like they were covered in sin and flames. Which, I suppose, they were. His particular brand of dislike extended to changing the prices on the food items to almost double when they came shopping. He did it in a clever way though, so clever I almost didn't notice.

On the receipt that he would tally up, he would make gross mathematical errors that could easily be missed if you didn't have a keen eye for math. I had a very keen eye for math, so keen that Ma pulled me from school at an early age. She said they had little to teach me that she couldn't teach me in half the time. I found the math errors almost instantly one morning peeking over his shoulder as he wrote up a receipt for one of the Main Street girls. My mouth was half way open to tell him the error, when something made me hesitate. The mistake was so obvious it had to be intentional, I realized, and a direct reflection of his attitude towards the women of the street.

After she'd left and the store was empty, I spoke up, "Do you do that to all the brothel women?" I asked. He hesitated and visibly stiffened.

"Do what now?" he asked, shuffling the receipts around, most likely to hide them from me and my prying eyes.

"Change the totals around, charge them more," I clarified. I set the broom aside for the moment, peeking at the receipts. He hurriedly filed them to the side.

"The prices are exactly as they appear in the store," he told me.

"I know," I pressed. "But when you do the math, it doesn't add up right. They pay almost twice what they should."

"I better not hear that come from your mouth again, hear? 'A false witness will not go unpunished, and he who breathes out lies will perish!'" He'd turned on me suddenly, wagging a finger menacingly at my face. I knew he didn't particularly dislike me or Heather, but I was sure having us underfoot all the time was a nuisance to him. It wasn't like he were particularly kind hearted, or I were godly enough to fit in with his family. Heather and I were good workers and he put up with us purely for that. This line of questioning was inappropriate, I realized, but my curiosity was too much.

"Yes, sir," I said, grabbing the broom again.

"This is why girls shouldn't get learned," he mumbled under his breath as he turned.

I felt the familiar itch at the end of my fingers, the same itch I felt when I fed Gloria the diarrhea and poisoned the miner. Ideas of how to get him back for speaking to me in such a manner brimmed in my mind, quick and unfettered. I had access to his entire apartment. What could I do that wouldn't be too obvious?

While I was in the mire of my own thoughts, Heather skipped in the front door of the shop, her wayward hair blowing around her. The manager may not have liked me, but he was more understanding of Heather. I'd seen his wife try to smooth her hair into something more manageable and even give Heather some hand me downs. Once, she even let Heather take the scraps from a project they'd been working on to make dresses for her dolls. If her husband died, Heather and I would be out of a home. We'd be entirely alone, and at square one again.

I decided to take my frustrations out on the dirty floor instead.

I remember the day I first saw *her* brighter than any other day. It was late March and only a week after I discovered the deceit of the store manager and his mathematics. It was a particularly beautiful, warm day that was so strange compared to what I knew of March in Kansas. There wasn't a hint of clouds in the sky and you could see down the slope of Cleopatra Hill all the way into the Verde Valley. If you squinted, I'm sure you could even see Clarkdale and the train. If you were especially quiet, the entirety of nature spoke to you.

I was sweeping the last bit of dust off the porch when I heard the clamor of noise that could only accompany the women of the night. Sure enough, when I shaded my eyes, I could make out the outline of four women in exquisite outfits sauntering down the street. The ruckus was to be expected—a mix of hostile threats and barely contained whistles. The dichotomy was the perfect analogy for Jerome.

They didn't split or break rank as they climbed the steps to the general store and barely even glanced in my direction. I averted my eyes... Until I saw her.

Her.

She had golden brown hair that caught the sunshine and reflected in the strangest, most pleasant of ways. She was taller than the others by nearly half a head, and with the stylish hat on her head, she stood even taller. Her eyes were a striking green—I could see that from where I stood—and outlined with a fashionable amount of kohl. She had a brief blush of freckles across her perfect nose, not the unceremonious dump my face had. Her outfit—it went without saying—was beautiful.

Never once did she turn to look at me, none of them did as they hurried into the store and spoke to each other in barely hushed tones, giggling. I set my broom aside and wandered in after them, passing through the shelves, trying to busy my hands as they picked through the shelves and collected items for purchase.

"My, my," came a voice that sounded hoarse and raspy.

When I turned, I was face to face with an ugly woman wearing the plainest face of the four women, her blonde hair in a heavy knot on top of her head. She spoke in a strange accent and resembled in more way than one a horse. I realized then she was referring to me, which was punctuated by her outstretched hand to touch a lock of my red hair that fell from the bonnet I always wore. "This is a color I could use," she said, twirling the lock in her fingers. Despite my better senses, I couldn't move, I was rooted to the spot. I could feel her hot breath on my face and see every bluish vein under her brown eyes. "What's your name, girl?" she pressed, releasing my hair.

"You get away from that girl, you whore," I heard the general manager growl from behind another shelf. He'd apparently been keeping a close eye on the women just as I had and saw the ugly one approach me. He stood in the most paternal way, his hands on his hips, his eyes narrowed down on the woman. The woman just laughed her hearty horse laugh, head back, making me jump with its sheer noise and power. The other three women joined their leader, flanking her in the standoff.

"I think we're about done here," she replied at long last, relishing the red that rose along his cheeks and face at her rebuke. They headed to the register and he nodded at me to go back to sweeping outside.

Moments later, the women emerged onto the porch. I saw her again and my breath caught in my throat, I nearly gasped. She turned then to look at me and her eyes met mine and everything—everything—in my body went hot and cold all at once.

"He overcharges you," I heard myself say before I could stop it.

They paused and the horse faced one turned to me, her eyebrow raised. "What did you say?" she asked.

I glanced around to make sure no one was near enough to listen in on our conversation. Through the window, I saw the manager disappear into the back room of the store. "He over-charges you. Do the math on the receipt. I noticed it last week." Nervous now, feeling my hands sweat, I chanced a glance from the horse faced woman to *her*. She was watching me with intensity, her hand curled under her jaw as she stared. Smiling. At me.

I felt my mouth go dry.

"What interesting information, we shall bring it up at our next purchase. Ladies," the horse woman turned to the others behind her and they descended the few steps on the porch. I watched them as they disappeared down the road to god knows where, then resumed sweeping to try to calm the racing thoughts in my brain.

Chapter 5

DESPITE WORKING ALL THE TIME, I still had a fair amount of tedium in my life. The days dragged on, as did my realization that my place at the general store was not long term. Once Heather became old enough to join society, or marry, I wouldn't be welcome anymore. I was allowed because I was an orphan raising my orphan sister. Once she became too old to truly be an orphan, my situation would become sad spinster. Marriage was out of the question for me (for numerous reasons), so I spent my time sorting through my skills to try for a trade.

On one hand, I could follow the path of my mother. Becoming a nurse wouldn't be too trying in these times, especially with my background. I knew enough from Ma to fall into swing quickly. Schooling would be an issue, but once Heather was old enough and married off, I could attend a school elsewhere. I didn't particularly miss Kansas, and I didn't consider Jerome my home, but I was hesitant to leave the smoldering ashes of my father and mother. I realized then that they were technically buried together, since Pa kept that little bit of her ashes on himself. This cooled my thoughts, and I decided on this path. At least they had each other, while I had neither.

In the meantime, though, I needed distraction.

Late at night after the general store switched to night crew and Heather was tucked into bed, I would sneak away and explore the streets of Jerome. It was a truly 24 hour town. The miner shifts were in 8-9 hour swings, always moving, always running. You'd think an 18 year old woman would stand out like a sore thumb in the night hours of a town, but I didn't. I was blissfully ignored and allowed to sink into relative anonymity. My clothes made it painfully obvious that I wasn't a sex worker, or at least not a decent one. I passed through the crowds with barely an eye turned in my direction. I'd taken to wearing bonnets, no matter how old fashion they were, to hide my hair color. In all the town I'd yet to see someone else with red hair as bright as mine and it often was the center of atten- tion. On those nights I wished to be as unremarkable as possible.

In those days, the brothels sat on the main strip. Years later, after sweeping reform and "civilization" came to Jerome, they would be thrown behind Main Street to "Husband Alley." It was a tossup for me; get lost in the crowd of Main Street or have relative secrecy down the quieter, emptier Hull Avenue? On most nights I stuck with Main Street, close enough to the object of my infatuation.

This particular night, I snuck around the side of Cathouse, a famed brothel that was arguably the most profitable of them all, and found my usual resting rock along the back. If I were careful, I could pace my way into the side alley and to the rock without a single person noticing. From here, I had easy view inside the windows into the parlor. No one bothered to curtain this window; it didn't show any fornication. No, this room was where the women sat and socialized with men, or simply with each other. The brothel could have been mistaken for a social ladies club if it weren't for their outfits. Despite the rich cloth most of the women wore about the town, skin was the true trade in the brothel. Their tight corsets were exchanged for loose tops, sliding off their shoulders and allowing their breast to hang freely. The skirts were sheer and sideswept, revealing long pale legs and bare feet.

I don't know what brought me time and time again to that rock and window without a single sight of sex, but I always found myself coming back. Sometimes, I would bring a snack stolen from the general store and eat while watching the conversation inside. Mostly, I was looking for *her*.

Tonight I didn't spot her, meaning, it was probably her night off. At one time, I thought I saw the long golden brown hair toppling over the edge of a chair, but I realized too late it wasn't her. I was nearly on my feet, edging closer to the window, trying to see anything.

Resigned, I picked up my meager things and edged my way around the side of the building, biding my time until the coast was clear enough to emerge from the shadows and join the sparse crowd back home. It was then that I heard the sniffle of a sob from the shadows to my side.

At first, I almost ignored the noise. It wasn't too uncommon to hear women crying in the streets of Jerome for one reason or another: A mining accident, a lost love, a miner or doctor or whoever promised to marry a woman and instead swore her off. There was the violence, too, for miners could be violent when they weren't tired as piss. I'd seen my share of women buying potions to cover their bruises from the apothecary across the street, which charged an inordinate amount of money for their goods.

The sob came again, so I adjusted my course to look as though I'd wandered from the street on accident and upon the girl. She was wearing a mix between fashionable clothes and parlor attire. Her corset was loose around her chest and her shirt was flowing and exposed her shoulders. Over it, she wore a fitted coat more befitting of the daytime, hastily buttoned and barely covering her in the evening March chill. Spring and summer seemed to be the predominate seasons in Jerome, and despite being only March, it wasn't cold enough to necessitate a full jacket at night. Still, she drew the jacket around herself in her misery.

"You alright, miss?" I called into the dark. The girl jerked, hastily wiping her eyes and peering through the darkness.

When she noticed that I wasn't one of the other workers, she softened and shook her head, waving me away. "Go on now, don't want your associations to drop with me." Her accent was foreign, her skin was so pale white she almost could glow in the dark. Her hair was jet black and straight, falling down her back and disappearing into the jacket.

I took another step toward her. "I've no associations to drop," I replied, a thrill starting in my stomach.

She paused and regarded me through her swollen eyes, considering. "You have a strange way of talk," she told me, scooting to the side to allow me room to sit on the low ledge next to her.

"So do you," I said, dropping down onto the ledge. "I'm from Kansas, I'm Louisa," I said.

"Veronica, from...well, everywhere. But mostly Britain." She said it with such strange punctuation I was enamored.

"That's awfully far from here," I allowed.

She shook her head, giving one final wipe of her eyes. "What are you doing in these shadows?" she asked me.

I shrugged and answered her question with a question. "What are you doing crying in the shadows?"

She didn't reply at first, and I figured she wouldn't answer me. Who would confide in a stranger? I was surprised when she spoke. "I'm pregnant," she whispered, then dropped her head into her hands. She didn't cry again immediately, but instead let the words wash over her in her abject misery.

"Are no congratulations in order?" I asked.

She barked a laugh from between her hands. "No, because it's only a matter of time before it becomes obvious and I am jobless, and a mother." The last words was bitter, spat out like a foul tasting fruit.

"Why don't you get rid of it?" I asked. The situation confused me. Back in Kansas, Ma had a box full of potions and herbs and medicines that would help women to get pregnant. That was the ultimate goal after marriage: get pregnant. Produce children to work the farm or carry on the name. Ma had a great record with her medicinal mixes and women trusted her more than the male doctor in town for midwifery. Rarely, though, a woman came to her pregnant and without a husband. In that case, she had other remedies that would end the pregnancy prematurely. I'd seen her give it to more than one woman—married and otherwise—over the years. She dealt with such secrecy though, no woman ever felt like they weren't in capable, silent hands. Of all things, Ma was capable and silent.

Veronica laughed at this, shaking her head. "In this town? They're so wicked, they all are, but they think going to church will clean their slate. There's no services like that here. We get what we deserve." The last bit was said so bitterly, so venomous, I leaned away from her slightly.

"No services?" I asked. "No nurse or doctor to give you the medicines?"

She shook her head. "Unless you know something I don't, I am done for."

I knew what I said next would have to be in great care. I felt the words form on my tongue and had plenty of time to stop them. If I did, maybe things would have been different. Maybe everything wouldn't have happened the way it did. Maybe, maybe, maybe.

"I do," I said.

Her eyes narrowed and she regarded me with marked skepticism. "What?" she asked.

"I do," I said, quicker now, licking my lips. "My Ma, she was a nurse back when we lived in Kansas. She had recipes and remedies like that."

"And I'm to just believe you?" she asked. I shrugged.

"There's only one way to find out." The girl watched me for a long minute, her gaze on my face, on the freckles across my nose and the extreme prominence of my chin. I watched her trace my broad forehead that protruded over my eyes. I knew what she saw. She was taking it all in, deciding if she should trust me or not. Whatever she saw solidified her decision.

"Tomorrow, then," she said, standing. "Here. This time. Don't be late." She disappeared into the brothel. I ran home, for once not caring that I was drawing attention to myself as I raced through the streets. I had a purpose. And I had a lot of work to do.

Chapter 6

THE WHOLE NEXT afternoon after work, I collected the various ingredients needed to make the potion for Veronica. I remembered everything with the same clarity I remember every moment with Ma in our kitchen. Once upon a time my only goal in life was to become just like her, absorbing her talents and skills. She taught me to create potions from the ingredients around the town. I missed her for the first time since moving to Jerome and burying her ashes in the graveyard at the base of the hill.

The biggest obstacle was knowing where to get everything. In Kansas, we grew most of the plants ourselves. Here? I didn't have the space for a garden and had no need for one until now. I slunk around gardens of homes all afternoon, recognizing the plants and herbs needed from our own garden back home. I wasn't even sure of the name of most of them; I recognized them on sight.

Heather returned from school and watched me curiously, wordlessly, as I assembled the ingredients and mashed them together in a pot I'd stolen from the general store below. After what seemed like forever, she disappeared into her room, then emerged holding a small book I recognized immediately.

I put the pestle down on the table slowly, watching her as she extended her hands and the book in it to me. "Where did you get that?" I asked. She didn't answer, but shook the book at me. "Heather, where did you get that?" I pressed again. She sighed, bringing the book to her chest.

"Ma gave it to me to hold before she died," she said softly. "She said it was important to the family. I think she knew you'd need it." She extended the book again, and this time I reached out to carefully take it from her.

The book was small, not much larger than the width of my palm. The cover was bare but worn, and inside held every potion, mix and recipe Ma had as a nurse. It covered common cures, potions she'd mixed, elixirs she'd used. She was rarely without the book and kept it protected in the breast of whatever coat she wore. Of course, I'd never forgotten about it, but I assumed that when Ma passed, it'd been with the rest of her things we abandoned in the train station that day. I figured it was lost forever, not hidden in Heather's things.

"I think you should keep it," she told me. Her voice was quiet for once. I brought the book to my own heart the same way she'd done only moments before and smiled at her. She turned then, skipping back into her room to change into something more freeing to run around with the neighborhood children. Once she was gone, I could finish the potion and use Ma's booklet as a guide to ensure all the ingredients were appropriate. Sure enough, it was exactly as I remembered it.

That night, I met Veronica in the same spot as before. I came early, hoping to catch sight of the golden haired girl, but Veronica was waiting for me. She was rocking on her toes, nervous, looking around. "You're sure this will work?" she asked me in her strange accent.

I nodded. "Drink 1/3 of it every night for three nights. You'll feel sick on the second day, and by the fourth day, it should be done."

She held the cocktail in her hand, regarding me skeptically. "And I won't perish?" she pressed. I shrugged.

"I don't think so. Would it matter if you did?" She seemed to like the honest answer and disappeared into the brothel without another word to me.

A week went by and I was disappointed by the return of my routine. I didn't realize how endless my days were until the excitement of the elixir. I didn't dare visit Main Street and peek in the windows again for fear of my potion not working. What if the potion killed Veronica? Or worse, what if it didn't work and Veronica chased me away? The later thought upset me because she would tell the rest of the women and my days of anonymously sneaking around the brothel were over. I decided to sit tight and, if no hellfire descended upon me, return in two weeks.

I didn't have to wait much longer. A week and two days went by before Veronica approached me. She sauntered into the general store, acting as if I didn't exist. Well, she was alive—that much was good news. She picked a random item and purchased it without saying a word to me. I went back to sweeping, disappointed. As she left, she hesitated at the rack next to me, extending a hand as though to examine something. Under her breath, she whispered to me, "Tonight." Nothing else. Her eyes wandered just a bit to make contact with mine so she knew I heard. I gave a little nod and went back to sweeping. She withdrew her hand and bustled out of the general store.

The rest of my afternoon was spent imagining what was going to happen. My guts turned over in my stomach, forcing my lunch to sit heavy and spoiled. I could barely contain my nerves (or excitement) as my shift came to an end. I still had hours to spend before the infamous 'tonight.' I assumed she meant the same time and place we'd met previously; what else could such an ominous statement mean?

I took the extra time to smooth my hair, which was so rarely touched, it was perpetually knotted and stuck together. The extra effort was rewarding, it looked glossy and clean despite rarely getting washed either. I didn't own makeup or anything to help hide the sea of freckles across my nose, so there was nothing to do there. I owned so little fashionable clothing that I didn't even have options on appropriate attire. I was left with my usual dated outfit and look, just with hair a little more polished than usual under my bonnet.

Night fell, and at the appropriate time, I slipped from my room and into the bustling street. Veronica was waiting for me again, but this time with the horse faced woman. She narrowed her eyes as she saw me, arms crossed over her chest. My heart skipped at the recognition in her eyes. The potion didn't work. It couldn't have worked. Why else would they look so serious?

"That's her," Veronica confirmed with a nod. I stopped a full six paces from them, frozen in the spot.

"I know ya," the horse faced woman said to me. "You're the girl from the general store, the one with that arse of an owner."

Veronica nodded. "That's where I found her. Took me nearly a week." They didn't try to advance on me, but for some reason, I was rooted to the spot, wanting nothing more than to run.

"Who taught you that potion?" asked the horse faced woman.

"My Ma," I managed, my voice shaky and broken. She nodded.

"How much for the recipe?" she asked. I shook my head. Her brows furrowed. "You don't have it? Or you won't sell it?" she pressed.

"I have it in my memory, and it's not for sale." She regarded me differently then, sizing me up.

"Very well." She reached into the pocket of her skirts and pulled out $5 worth of cash. "This will do, then, until we need you again?" She extended the cash to me. I'd seen $5 before at the store, and once or twice dropped off a similar amount to the landlord when we all lived in the box on the other side of Jerome. But $5 to myself? With no rent to pay and no one to owe? I closed the gap between us and took the money in my hand, baffled.

"Might do well to buy yourself some better clothes," she said. Veronica laughed. I realized it was a mean statement made at my expense but I didn't particularly care. I was basically rich off one potion.

"Until you need me again?" I asked.

The horse faced woman laughed. "Ever since the doctor was chased out by them religious folk, we haven't got anyone to help us with these matters. It's bad for business. This...this is good for business. You better keep some handy. In fact, come back when you got some more. I'll buy it all off you." She nodded, pleased with this suggestion and turn of events. I considered her offer. I wanted to accept it on the spot but I knew enough from watching Pa's negotiations not to just accept an offer blindly.

"$7 a potion," I said quickly. "And I won't sell to no one else." She considered this a moment, then nodded.

"Quite the business woman. I accept your offer." She extended a wrinkled, rough hand and shook mine. "If you ever find that general store lacking, I could use a good girl here," she told me.

I shook my head. "I've no desire," I said.

She laughed then, her bray echoing through the streets. I turned to look to see if anyone noticed us there, if they were aware of our highly illegal bartering. "Honey, I couldn't sell you at a discount," she said, sympathetic almost. Veronica didn't join in on the laughter, she just frowned and went inside. The lady with the horse face turned to go back into the house, then paused. "What's your name, girl?" she asked.

"Louisa," I replied.

"Louisa," she echoed, nodding. "Midwestern name. I'm Jennie, I own this place. When I said I could use a good girl , I meant a girl about business, a girl who knows math. You think things through, alright? Really think on it." I nodded, though I was sure I would never drop to such a low. The general store was not a forever situation, but it was something to pass the time until I could go apprentice with a doctor to become a nurse like Ma. This side money would help pay for tuition and maybe help move Heather and I out of the general store. Now that I had to make all the potions, I needed a space for a garden, I couldn't steal supplies from yards and keep mixing potions in our small bedroom.

I walked slowly through the streets back to the general store, contemplating all the things I would need to help my enterprise. With $5 in my pocket, I had a good place to start.

. . .

Business was booming, truly. My savings (which previously had been $0) exploded as my need for a true garden grew. I considered my options; stay working for the general store or move out and become independent. As a single woman moving out was unheard of. Jerome was by no means progressive but certain allowances were made for women there over Kansas. The more I learned about the brothel women, the more I realized the owners of the brothel were some of the richest women in the territory. Some of the married women were richer than their husbands because of their own business savvy.

I intended to utilize mine.

The biggest obstacle that stood in my way was the fact that my doings were entirely illegal. Arizona was a territory and Jerome just a small city, but law was law. If anyone in the city found out that I was growing herbs (or stealing them from gardens) for the purpose of ending pregnancy for brothel women... Well, that would be the end of a lot of things for me. It's one thing to be a sex worker, another to own them, and an entirely other to aid them in their wrongdoing. If I were to keep up my secret endeavors, I needed a cover. The general store was ideal for this, no matter how much I was growing to hate it.

Still, my garden space was a serious consideration. I settled on purchasing a small lot of land not too far from the general store, but well enough off the beaten path for no one to intrude. It was close enough to some homes and other gardens to be very inconspicuous. Additionally, I started my garden with stolen clippings (starting from seed would have been impossible to keep up with the demand) so any true attention to my garden would be catastrophic. I spent most of my time off tilling the soil and managing it.

This posed a problem with the manager of the general

store. Heather didn't understand the extent of what I was doing, but assumed it required secrecy. Ma operated under much the same rules. True, her role as a nurse was known all through our home in Kansas, but if anyone truly knew the extent of her underground potions business, we would have been run out long before consumption did it for her.

The manager was busy enough not to intrude completely. He'd seen me once or twice return from tilling my garden, covered in dirt and soot and made a reproachful noise. After getting caught for the third time, I decided to give my own explanation. The last thing I needed was for him to draw his own conclusions and fire me for it. Not that I needed the money, but I did need the cover.

"My Ma started a garden before she passed," I lied, partially. "I hadn't the heart to tend to it, but now I do. I can bring you some fresh produce if you'd like?" He declined the offer, looking mollified for the moment. He was more shrewd than any other person I'd met and I knew the front wouldn't last long, or he'd find some other reason to get rid of me. He'd been making off comments about wanting to expand his own housing with his income and made it very clear he wanted to turn our little guest apartment into something for himself. I wondered how he'd ever hire someone else; he paid so little that without the housing incentive, surely no one would work there.

Through all this, while I collected my cash in the small box I shoved in the bottom of a suitcase, I realized how futile this was. I was saving money for what? For nursing school? Would I ever go? I sat on the edge of the bed in the tiny little corner room Heather and I shared when I heard a creak of the floorboard. Heather stood before me, her eyes wide as she stared at the overflowing cash pile in my hands.

"Oh," she said.

"I know," I responded, feeling the heat rise up in my face. "I don't know what to do with it," I told her. She nodded and sat down next to me on the bed. Her hair was less wild today than normal, pulled back into a semi-secure knot behind her head. Still, as she leaned close to me, the bits of hair tickled my face. She extended a hand slowly to touch the money, run her fingers over it, examining the feel. "It's okay," I urged. She picked it up and ran it through her hands—coins, dollars, other strange assortments.

"I'm afraid to touch it for long," she said to me. She understood the situation more intimately than I could have thought for a girl her age.

"I'm afraid to get caught," I replied. She nodded and replaced the money carefully, folding her hand in her lap.

"He'll know," she said, referring to the general manager of the store.

"He will," I agreed. We both stared at the money some more.

"It's not just for me," I said at last, misinterpreting her silence. "It's for us."

She nodded slowly. "For us how?" she asked. My silence answered that question.

"Until he finds out, I guess." We were silent again.

I considered counting the money daily from that point on. Would Heather tell anyone? Would I be in any sort of danger? These thoughts plagued me until I discovered an easy solution —the bank. It had been created fairly recently in Jerome but I did not trust it. I decided to make the trip down to Clarkdale the next day to deposit some of the money under a fake name. I'd keep some on me at all times in case there was an emergency, and some hidden in the garden. The more evenly I distributed the wealth, the less likely it were to be stolen or misused. The plan worked well—some in the bank (under the alias Goldy Lockwood, which I invented on the spot), some buried in a box in the garden, some under my clothing, and some on me at all times. It burned a hole in my chest to feel that small wad pressed gently up against my breast.

I don't know why I felt compelled to, but I also bought some fabric while in Clarkdale. Buying new clothes outright would surely point out my newly found wealth to the grocer. Fabric could be cheap, and as far as anyone knew, it was free or stolen. I delivered this to Heather in an attempt to buy her silence, telling her to make clothes for herself. To my surprise, she made some clothes for me, too, and for the first time since moving to Jerome, we were outfitted in new clothing.

Chapter 7

THE ONE YEAR anniversary of our move to Jerome also signaled the one year anniversary of Ma's death. The general manager, who knew very little details about her death, allowed me the day to travel down the hill to the cemetery with Heather and pay our yearly respects. Neither of us had visited in the year, and the trip was sober and quiet.

While we stood over her grave, a flash out of the corner of my eye caught my attention. There, just a few grave stones down, stood *her*. She wore the most fabulous turquoise waistcoat with a fashionable hat that covered her eyes and face from the summer sun. Heather and I suffered under our old bonnets and piecemeal fashion while she looked radiant and perfect. She held flowers close to her chest, unaware of our existence.

I hadn't seen her much in the weeks since I started working with the brothel. I often wondered if any of the potions I made touched her soft, pink lips. The idea thrilled me in ways I couldn't describe. The women of the brothel decidedly avoided the general store, partly out of respect for my privacy (I hoped) and partially due to my shedding light on their financial unfairness. If they came at all, it was to buy a single item, slip me a note or whisper a word to me, and disappear out the door.

She looked up then, making eye contact with me, and my head jerked back quickly to look at Ma's grave. Heather watched me quizzically as I obviously side eyed her, head straight forward to look at Ma's grave. "They're everywhere these days," Heather whispered up to me. I shrugged, feeling sweat collect under my lip. Out of the corner of my eye, I could see her figure move, and I realized with horror that she was headed toward us. "Miss Nelson says they're a stain on this earth," she continued, her voice just loud enough for me to hear. Her whispers were conspiratorial, though, so if she were looking at us, she would know.

"Louisa." It was her.

I turned my head slowly, feeling my throat dry and jaw clench, all sense leaving my body. Heather's jaw visibly dropped next to me, her eyes narrowing in a way only a child's could do. I met her gaze full on, blinking hard. "Yes?" I replied. She offered me a small smile, almost coy, her head tilted.

"Is this your darling sister?" she cooed. Heather frowned in response.

"Yes," I responded, aware suddenly those were the only words I'd spoken to her.

"She looks nothing like you," she said. I wasn't sure if that were a compliment to Heather or just a plain statement. We really didn't look a thing alike, especially with Heather's wild brown hair and her skin the color of the mountains from being in the sun all day. I still hadn't found a way to prevent sun burn, only a way to placate the pain with aloe. I found a bit in Ma's book about it and created a salve I carried almost everywhere with me. "What brings you to the cemetery?" she asked when I didn't respond.

"To see a grave," Heather retorted, as though it were the most obvious thing ever. "Just like you," she added, craning her neck to look toward the grave she'd just walked away from. It's then I realized I didn't even know *her* name.

She sidestepped to place herself directly in front of Heather's view of her grave. Her smile was fake and forced, stretching her face in an unnatural way that just made her beauty more obvious. She was beautiful in the way a colorful snake was beautiful—a predatory warning, a sleight of hand to distract. "Clever girl. You'll make quite a splash in the world with those brains," her reply was curt, her eyes leveled on me. I felt my throat dry and forced a swallow. "I don't think we've ever formally met," she said, her smile turning. "I've heard all about you, Louisa. I'm Tabitha." She extended a hand then, soft and delicate behind those beautiful, expensive gloves with the intricate pattern on them. I could see Heather's eyes widen from the corners of my vision, focusing on those gloves. I extended my own hand with the dirt under my nails and the dried leaves from gardening that morning. She took it none the less and gave it a mild squeeze.

"I must be off," she said, tossing an unpinned portion of her hair back over her shoulder. "I'm sure we'll meet again," her voice was cryptic and she ended with an exaggerated wink, before flouncing off up the road.

"What was that? How did she know who you were?" Heather demanded, her eyes flickering back and forth through the cemetery to see if anyone noticed. "We'll be out of a home if *he* finds out," she hissed in a loud whisper.

I raised my hand to silence her, shaking my head. "We haven't a thing to worry about. I'm not...I'm not working there. At least not like that. It's..." I tried to pull the word from the air.

"Bad," Heather finished.

I shrugged, gathering my sleeves around me. I was sweating in the heat but refused to roll up a sleeve and expose my skin to the sun to burn. I frowned. "It's what we have to do. It's only a matter of time before they kick us out. We can't live there forever. We can't go back to Kitty's, and I'd never be able to afford a real place for us to live otherwise. You understand this, don't you?"

Heather was silent as she stared at the ground. She picked at the sleeve of her new blouse, made from the fabric I bought, and considered this. "Yes, but I don't like it." She began to walk out of the cemetery without looking back to see if I was following. I followed close behind her, hesitating only to look at the grave stone that Tabitha had been looking at. There was no name, just a date—February 6th 1984-February 7th 1984. An infant. I paused longer than I intended to, then hurried after Heather up the hill.

———

A tense silence settled around Heather and I until I had a day off from working, in which I enticed her to visit the new picture show. They'd built the theatre a few years before but burnt down in the fire and took that long to rebuild. The history of the multiple fires hung like an oppressive lightning storm over Jerome, waiting to strike again. What confused me was the structure of all the housing and businesses, all made of wood. For a place so concerned with a fire ending their entire livelihood again, they sure did use flammable material. I thought of the brick buildings in the towns I saw on the train ride out here and wondered why.

The picture show was a new addition as of 1896 and

bustling with the afternoon crowd. All around us, I saw families and groups of people I didn't recognize, though Heather knew quite a few of them. She skipped from group to group, saying her hellos to the families and the kids. I picked at a scab on my forearm from tending to my garden.

"Louisa!" came a voice I vaguely recognized. It was the woman who lived next to the garden I purchased. She was plump and friendly and of a part of society that didn't encourage women to work. I saw her on occasion and made a good enough excuse for having a garden not attached to housing, an excuse that eluded me at the moment. She smiled her wide smile as she scuttled over to Heather and me, nodding. "Remarkable how your garden is holding up in this heat," she said, winded by the distance she traveled. "Absolutely remarkable. Much like this picture show, isn't it? I heard about them buildin' this months ago and I was flabbergast. Flabbergast! Can you imagine somethin' so fancy right here in Jerome? My, as a settlement we've really grown." She shivered then, though if it were from excitement or something else I couldn't tell.

"Yes," I managed a word in, offering up a smile. Heather held my hand absently and looked up at the plump woman with wonder.

"Oh! And who is this?" she asked, kneeling down ever so slightly to speak to Heather eye to eye. Her size didn't allow her to do much moving, though, so she simply bent over partially.

"Heather, her sister," Heather said slowly, unsure. She glanced up at me again.

"Yes, this is my younger sister, Heather."

"I had no idea you had any kin!" she cried. Heather flinched visibly at the comment.

"Just us since Pa died in February, no ma'am," Heather replied, a bit tart.

The woman clearly didn't know that she'd said anything to upset and paled visibly. "Oh my word! Oh my WORD! I...I had no idea..." she shook her head and placed a hand on Heather's shoulder. I suppose it was meant to be in comfort, but really it served only to make Heather uncomfortable. Neither of us particularly liked to be touched by anyone but each other, and even then, it only extended to holding each other's hands in situations like this. Heather was growing out of that quickly, holding my hand less and less frequently in public. I expected her to drop it any minute now.

"It's quite all right," I cut in to stop her rampant rambling. She still seemed peeved by the mistake.

"Why don't you girls stop by after the picture show? For some lunch, yes?"

I glanced down at Heather and saw the look in her eye. "I'm afraid we have other plans, perhaps another time?" I offered. "It's such a kind offer of you, offering food to orphans such as ourselves," I added. She was mollified by this and nodded, reassured that she was indeed so kind.

"Come by on Sundays after noon any time to play cards. We've quite a group, you'd be welcome." She made her good-bye's then, disappearing into the crowd to join her husband or friends or whomever else she were with.

"Who was that?" asked Heather.

"A woman who lives next to the garden I maintain. I see her sometimes."

"Does she know why you have a garden?" Heather asked between clenched teeth.

"Partially, I have a farce. I don't recall it now, but it was passable. She's of high society, we should take her up on her offer one day," I retorted. Heather considered this as the line started moving to file into the picture show.

"She must think we're high society, with a garden and seeing the picture show."

I offered a subtle shrug of my shoulders. "Perhaps. Or we've some inheritance and no income; it doesn't matter. It would suit us to align with her, I think," I told her.

She considered this herself and then nodded. "Yes, I need to find a job soon."

"You need no such thing," I said, my tone sharper than I intended. "I have the means," I followed up softly. "You need your education," I pressed.

Heather shook her head. "No, I need to be helping you. You didn't go to school as long as I have and you're smarter than all my teachers. I don't need the schooling. My skill is mending clothes and knitting. I can be employed quickly, I know it."

I squeezed her hand almost painfully until she cried out. "You will stay in school until you are finished with your education. That is the end of it." I looked down and saw that she was pouting with tears welling up in her eyes, threatening to spill over. She was making every effort to contain them as we took our seats in a row of bench seats.

She didn't speak to me the rest of the day.

Part of the way through the picture show, I was aware of eyes on me. I chanced a glance out of the corner of my eye and saw Tabitha, sitting with a group of women of the night. They had wide berth, as many of the families and women did not sit near them at all. It made for cramped quarters on either side, but they didn't seem to mind. They spread out in an unlady-like fashion, stretching their bodies in a way that Heather and I dared not. Tabitha's eyes weren't on the picture show at that moment; they were on me. I chanced a full glance in her direction and was shocked to see her meet my eyes and raise an eyebrow. I shot my gaze back to the screen, feeling my heart rate rise and the sweat begin to collect on my palms. When I looked again, she was still staring, but this time offered the slightest of waves. I glued my eyes to the screen and refused to look again.

Was that malice in her eyes? Or was it something more? I replayed the look on her delicate face, with that soft upturned nose and simple, delicate freckle pattern so different from mine. It made my stomach drop just thinking about it.

Chapter 8

IT DIDN'T TAKE LONG for my prediction about the general store to come true. It was less than a week after the picture show when the general manager called me into his office. He wore a heavy frown as he instructed me to sit. I felt claustrophobic in the small place, acutely aware that I was locked in an office with a man many years my senior. He didn't seem to share my discomfort, much less notice it.

"Louisa, I'm sorry to tell you this, but we're in no need of your employment anymore. Times are changing and I've got to convert the building. The new homes along the hill are coming up, and the women of society need their things delivered. We need boys who can drive a carriage to deliver these goods to them. For this reason, we're replacing you with boys who can operate a carriage." He said this and watched me expectantly.

I suppose I could have begged for my job. I could have sworn to learn to ride or drive or whatever else he was asking of me. For once, my urban upbringing was not helping me. If I'd grown up on a farm like the others, I might have had a skill to contribute. As of now, I had no skills to help with this change of business and I was too tired to care.

"And we are out of home as well, I suppose?" I asked. He was taken aback by my forced casual tone. I suppose I was partially upset by the prospect of finding a new home and relocating our meager things in such short notice, but really, I was glad. I'd been looking at the housing further up the hill where the high society lived. I realized I could lie and say we had an inheritance that was delayed on account of our fathers death or something. I could make up any assortment of non-truths and they would believe me. In a town so new—not even a town yet, or a city, just a settlement—I could be anyone. Sure, I was recognizable by my hair color but how important was that? They'd know I had a garden, I used to work in the general store, and on one fateful day a year prior, I stumbled into town with my Pa and little sister. In a settlement of immigrants, I was just another body.

Except, of course, the sex workers. They knew what I did with that garden.

"Yes, but I will make allowances. You have two weeks to find new housing and new employment. That is all. You are allowed to finish out your duties the next week, but I shan't pay you for the second week." He paused then. "You'd do best to be out *quickly*." There was an emphasis on the words I didn't quite expect and for a minute, I wondered if he knew. A longer look in his face told me he didn't. He looked sorry, sad almost, not the look of a man firing an employee for helping the brothel. For making soups and potions to end the life of an unborn child. No, he couldn't mask that sort of hatred. It didn't matter if my services were to mend a cold, heal a cut, fix a bruise... I would still be tainted in his eyes by associating with the women. I was still helping *them*.

"Thank you," I said, standing and turning to the door. He didn't say anything, much less pursue me as I left the building and walked the steps down the general store into the street. I was surprised to feel a smile stretch across my face, wide and free.

I considered going to Heather's school to tell her the good news, when I realized she wouldn't be nearly as thrilled as I was. She was so sullen these days, playing rarely if ever with the kids in the neighborhood. Instead, she'd busy herself with mending clothing and organizing the fabric swatches I'd bring to her. I knew she would leave school before I was ready to let her, with or without my permission. It wouldn't surprise me if she had a similar operation as I did—secretly constructing pieces to sell to anyone who would buy.

Instead of going to her, I decided to walk amongst the camps and housing I considered purchasing. Should I sell the garden and move it to a new home? Or would I risk too much keeping the plants so near to home? I realized then that I shouldn't mix business and home, and set about looking at the small homes that dotted the hillside until the sun began to set, then returned to the general store to tell Heather the news.

As expected, she wasn't thrilled. "WHAT?" she hissed, dropping her things to the ground in a show of her infamous temper tantrums. They'd become few and far between in the year since we'd lost Ma. She was still a 15 year old girl, torn from her home and forced to move to an entirely different way of life. We might as well have been on the sun for all she understood and cared.

"We knew this would happen," I reasoned, reaching out to her. I knew better than to touch her, and even the motion of my hand toward her made her recoil violently. "And I've been looking at places we can move to. Up on the hill. We can see the valley, and we can get a place for you to have a shop to work out of. We can figure it out. And if you want to contribute to the income, I won't force you back to school."

She stopped her temper tantrum then, watching me carefully. "I don't have to go back to school?" she pressed. I shook my head. She sighed and dropped to the ground, tears streaming down her face. "Good, I hate that place," she whispered.

I felt that unpleasant sensation of my stomach aching and felt heat flush over my face. "You love school?" I asked, or said, I wasn't quite sure with my inflection.

She shook her head and wiped the tears with the back of a soiled hand that caused a streak of mud and dirt. "I used to, now the kids are mean to me because I'm not pretty. And because we're poor."

"Not anymore," I said. "We'll say we came upon an inheritance. That when I lost my job, we reached out to family and found we'd inherited from a recently deceased aunt. Wired it to us." I was nodding at this new plan which sounded much better and more believable than my previous one. What miner had money? At least money that wasn't spent on drink or whoring.

Heather stopped crying then and looked up at me. "Yes," she said slowly, and nodded. "It scares me how you can lie so easily, Louisa," she added. "Don't ever lie to me." It wasn't a question; it was a demand. It was a cold fact we decided on at that moment.

I sat down on the floor opposite of her and extended my hand as though we were making an agreement. "I will never lie to you, Heather," I said. She took my calloused, worn hand in her own and shook it mildly.

"I've been making potions for the prostitutes to get rid of

their babies. They pay me $7 a batch, and I make a lot of batches." The words fell out of my mouth quickly and before I had much time to consider what she may think. Her eyes widened and she leaned back, regarding me differently. "I do other things, too. Like medicine and herbs for coughs and sores... that's not..."

"Seven dollars?" she whispered, interrupting. "A batch? That's..." she looked up to the ceiling and considered.

"We're not rich," I quickly interrupted her thinking. I'd done the math time and time again, backwards and forwards in my head. I knew what I had down to the penny. "But we can manage. And if you help, then we'll be almost rich. We can be society ladies, self-made. Yeah?" She nodded then, her tears replaced with a smile. In an uncharacteristic show of affection, she threw her arms around my neck and hugged me close. "Let's find a place to live tomorrow. It's too small for us here. Just promise me you'll stop when you have enough to go to school and get out of here for good."

I promised.

Heather and I moved to the outskirts of the hill less than a week later without saying another word to the general manager. I collected my last pay and gave him no inclination on where we were heading. His wife appeared a little concerned on that front, inquiring after Heather about what we planned to do. She kept silent as a church mouse, giving little more than a heavy shrug as she collected the last bits of her sewing material.

The hill was beautiful in comparison to the hustle and bustle (and dirt and horse manure) of living on Main Street. Here, the streets were silent except for the play of children, and the view was of the magnificent Verde Valley. The lack of stifling dust from wagons and noxious fumes of the excrement filled street only moved to improve our disposition. Heather set to work in her tiny bedroom turned office creating clothes for both of us and to sell. She solicited her services up and down the hill and, quickly, became the local seamstress for the women who didn't have the time to travel to Clarkdale or talent to do it themselves. She opened her office to private lessons within a week of moving, teaching those years older than her how to mend and sew.

The first month we lived on the hill was peaceful and serene. Summer was fading away in its slow, undetectable manner and 1897 was creeping up on us. My 19th birthday came and passed. In Arizona, the summer didn't quite end until well into October or November, with the days becoming shorter and the temperatures dropping at such a slow rate it was nearly undetectable. First thing in the morning was brisk and bright, but warmed considerably by noon. My garden began its transition into the winter plants, which was less concerning than in Kansas. I could grow almost all my plants year around, I realized, and capitalized on this. I began to grow more than just herbs and included vegetables and considered adding trees. The soil wasn't quite rich enough for that, so I paced myself.

Maybe someday. Maybe we'd stay.

A little over a month passed before I had any visitors. It was a cool afternoon in November when a knock on the door caused Heather to rise from her sitting place and answer it, her tone biting as she said, "May I help you?"

I came behind her to see the horse faced woman, Jennie, standing in our doorway. She looked approvingly at our little house, nodding her head. "Not too bad for a meager salary," she whistled under her breath. I rushed her inside with a quick wave of my hands, looking either way down the street to ensure no one saw her at our door. The street was blissfully empty.

"What is it you want?" I asked, hands on my hips. Heather retreated a step behind and crossed her arms over her chest.

"I've just come to call," Jennie said, unbuttoning her gloves. "Looks like you've made quite a bit of yourself. Two orphans without a penny to their name, now living on the hill." She nodded to herself. "You remind me of myself when I was your age. I came to Arizona with one thing in mind; to make my own way. It takes a certain...woman...to climb to the top in a land like this. Lawless. Daring." Her smile was introspective, a bare finger tapping her bottom lip as she considered her words. "I had to do a little research. It wasn't hard to trace your lot up here and see what you'd created. The true American dream, really." I couldn't tell if her words were appreciative or mocking. I decided not to reply.

"I asked you once if you wouldn't like to join me in business, and you declined. I've had a sudden opening I need filled, and I need it filled by a woman with savvy. I need someone who will get things done, and punish those who deserve it." That smile became a thin line of barely contained anger. I was curious but didn't dare press the matter. I'd learned through the year that silence is the best way to keep others talking. They often find it so uncomfortable they need to fill it with something, even if it's their own downfall.

"The position will be part time. It's balancing books, keeping an eye on the transactions, ensuring there's no...funny business," her mouth curved painfully around the words. Funny business. I'd never heard that phrase before. "Can I trust you to do that? I've seen your way with numbers first hand." She was referring to my catching the slight from the general store manager, as she had no other time to assess my mathematical skills. Well, except haggling for a higher price for my potions.

"What of my reputation?" I asked. She laughed and fanned herself with her glove. "Oh, you're a woman, you will always have a reputation. I am invited to play cards with the ladies on the weekends, and I am invited to the soirees and to dine with the rich. You know what they say about me when I am not around? I peddle flesh, I am a demoness, a witch. You know what they say of other rich women in other fields? The same, just variations on it. A woman with power, a woman with money, a woman without a man is a scourge no matter what her trade. You can choose to sit in this box on a hill the rest of your life or you can join the elite. It's up to you." She slid her gloves back on and turned to the door.

I could see Heather appraise her outfit with envy.

I could feel the thin walls of the house, the lowly location on the base of the hill, the distance between where we were and where we could be. I could feel the impossibility of going to nursing school slip through my fingers every day, a dream I realized I'd never truly had. It was just another place to go when this inevitably ran out.

"I'll give you a week to come to your senses. You know where to find me," she tossed a final look over her shoulder before letting herself out and leaving Heather and I shrouded in silence.

Chapter 9

WE ARGUED FOR DAYS. Heather was resolute in her childish ways that I avoid any further associations with *those* women. She frowned perpetually over what I was doing thus far and reminded me endlessly of the goal: nursing. She wanted nothing more than for me to become a true, real, nurse like Ma was. I didn't press the issue and upset her delicate notion of what Ma really was, that I'd gotten these recipes from her. She remembered a loving source of endless light, whereas my memories were more realistic. Ma sold potions that were controversial in nature as a side project to keep the money flowing when Pa fell behind on his carpentry.

One night, I overheard them fight over that very subject. Pa was war torn about her side projects and her little book of what he called "Black Magic." More than once, I heard Pa call Ma a witch because of what she did in the shadows. Heather either willfully forgot these exchanges or was totally oblivious to the tension that occasionally hung in our house before Ma got sick.

Pa truly loved Ma, I knew that. But there was a sort of relief about her coming down with consumption and us forced to leave Kansas for newer shores. I'm sure Pa planned on keeping her from ever using that little book ever again. He'd roll over in his grave to see his eldest daughter pick up the trade after his wife died.

There was no middle ground with Heather, but I only had a few days to make a decision. I wanted more. The fine linens that Heather made were fair enough (better than our dirt worn and torn clothing from Kansas) but I lusted for the elegant look of the ladies of the high society. The catch was they'd never invite me if they knew my origins. An orphan. Working at a general store to make ends meet. Mixing potions that end pregnancies for the whores of Main Street. They'd laugh me out of their circles. Even an inheritance from an aunt wasn't enough; she had no name for us to cling to.

Heather knew what my decision would be. I just didn't expect to wake up one morning and see all of her things packed and gone, her bedroom empty, and all the money I kept in the house gone. I was thankful then for my multiple stashes in the bank, under a pseudonym, and buried in the garden. She'd taken a small enough portion not to affect me directly but large enough to be on her own. I didn't know where she'd go, but she was 15 and nearly an adult. She could make her own decisions.

And I made mine.

That afternoon, I made the short hike down the hill to Main Street and knocked on the front door of Jennie's Birdhouse. She answered, smiling that awful smile on her horse face. "Come in," she said, without a hint of surprise. She'd been expecting me.

I'd never been inside the brothel and peeking into the windows did nothing to prepare me. The carpet was rich and clearly imported from somewhere far away and made me want to take my dirty shoes off. She lead me around the side of the house, past the furniture I'd seen through the windows. As the daughter of a carpenter, I was acutely aware of how well-made everything was and how expensive it must have been. The wood was unlike any material I'd seen in the area, sturdy and strong. It smelled a like Pa.

We wound around the side of the main parlor and into a set of offices away from the bustle of the main floor. We were close enough to hear most of the commotion without it being overwhelming. It was mid-day so the noise was basically nonexistent. An occasional man would wander in to find his company, but for the most part, the busiest time was at night. The brothel was open 24 hours, seven days a week to accommodate the around the clock schedule the miner's had.

"This will be your office," Jennie said, leading me to the second door on the right. It was barely larger than a broom closet but held a desk just as fine as the furniture outside. Despite how cramped it was, I could feel my heart soar in my chest at the thought of having my own space. Sure, I had my own bedroom in our small house...but this? I gave Heather the front room, the largest of them all, for her office and to allow her to work. This was my own space where I would...I wasn't even sure. I ran my fingers over the top of the desk, feeling the firm wood beneath my hands.

"You're welcome to join us for suppers, lunches, and breakfasts. Most of the women live here, or at least rent a room out for their purposes. You'll be balancing the books of all my brothels, not just this one. I'm the Madam of three through town, and one down in Cottonwood. I don't see that one as much, you'll have to go there once a month to connect with the bookkeeper there. It goes without saying that it's necessary to have multiple people run the books."

She motioned to the chair behind the desk, allowing me to sit behind my own desk. It felt like a throne. It took every ounce of my will to keep a stupid smile off my face. There was something so right about it.

"This job isn't without its challenges," she said, steepling her fingers. She'd seated herself at a chair opposite my desk, leaning back to stretch her legs in front of her like a man. "See, our last girl...well, she came up short on some funds. Taking a little off the top. Thought we wouldn't notice. But I always notice." She let the last phrase hang in the air for a moment longer than the rest of her words. It was a point I understood. "And collecting from the girls can be a problem sometimes. You'll soon learn who is chronically late, who is chronically early, and who spends most of their earnings on booze." Her smile was slow and wicked. "Not to say that I disapprove of these vices, but money must be paid. The consequences are as stands—two strike rule. That goes for all my employees. There's no need for secrecy in public about your relationship with us, but I won't advertise it neither. Your affairs are your affairs." She said that last bit the same way she said, "but I always notice," as though she was making a point.

"Now, I'll leave you to familiarize yourself with the paperwork. There's a bit of a backlog, it'll keep you busy." She stood then, turning to leave. Before going too far, she hesitated at the door and looked over her shoulder. "And we'll do something about your wardrobe at a later time. I'll send someone." Her frown was the last thing I saw as she shut the door behind her and left me to the piles of paperwork.

Two days went by before I saw anyone outside of my office. The paperwork that was left was in handwriting that must have been from someone missing a finger or some other ailment, because it was incomprehensible. I spent most of the first day trying to decipher the texts, and the rest of the time sorting through the mass of finances.

It didn't take me long to find the skimming off the top that occurred, much less the undeniable fact that Miss Jennie was one of the richest woman in the entire Arizona territory. Between her brothels, the estates, the saloon she owned...she easily owned a fourth of Jerome. The skimming went on for so long I truly doubted Jennie caught it, more like the skimmer implicated themself somehow.

Her girls were also wealthy by comparison to Pa's miner salary. It took me awhile to figure out the cost of each of their services and what they meant. Different women were paid different amounts for the same acts, mostly, I assumed, based on their talent or looks. I noticed that some of them worked less than others but made quite a bit more. The secret was the drink; the alcohol pulled most of their income in the way of a tab. The business model was profoundly simple but also ingenious—get every man stinking drunk and charge him per act, not per minute or hour, and collect on that *and* the booze.

It'd been two days of nearly 12 hours a day working until the night got too rowdy to concentrate. I took a long lunch to tend to the garden and eat a meal, not confident enough yet to join the women in their morning or afternoon (much less evening) meals.

"So much work," came a smooth voice, and I looked up to see Tabitha standing in the doorway. She wore her typical predatory smirk, as though she wanted to pounce on me at any moment. I felt the heat rush to my pale face, probably outlining the freckles like the sore spots they were.

"Pardon me?" I asked, trying to look like I wasn't absolutely perturbed by her presence.

"I said, so much work," she repeated, her smile unchanged. She gently pushed herself off the doorway she'd been leaning against (so casual I could have sworn it was intentional) and closed the short distance to my desk, leaning forward and placing her palms flat on the surface. I could see every vein in her exposed hand, not hidden behind gloves like in the graveyard. Her fingers were long and delicate without an ounce of dirt under her nails. I still had the rings of my gardening work evident on my skirt and my hands. I hurried to tuck them away from her view.

"You need a reprieve, and Miss Jennie demands we fix your attire." She allowed a quick raking of her gaze up and down the visible parts of my outfit. Old, dirty, sweat stained...I was sure I looked every bit the orphan I was. "And, hopefully, your hygiene." A giggle floated up from behind her and Veronica peeked her head around the corner, dressed in a similarly splendid outfit. "Come, little one, be our doll for the day." She flashed a smile so quick I almost missed it. It was so different from the crying girl I saw all those months ago on the porch. A cruel comment died on my lips as she assessed me without obvious disgust.

They lead me upstairs to the bathing house and demand I sit in the tub and scrub until all hints of dirt were removed from my body. I did so demurely, insisting they leave the bathhouse. "Does nudity irk you?" asked Tabitha.

"No," I replied quickly, too quickly.

"Because your choice in career is quite questionable in the face of that." Both girls tittered, but left me to myself to bathe fully. They handed me soaps and concoctions that I'd never seen before that turned my skin paler than I expected from cleanliness. The assault of smells made my eyes water and my stomach lurch. I rinsed my hair time and time again until it ran clean and lathered it with exotic scents that I couldn't even place. Some scents—lavender, rose, vanilla—I could pull from my garden. The rest were foreign and made my skin tingle delightfully.

The water of the bath was warmer than any bathing I'd ever done. I sunk into the deep tub, letting the dirty water settle below my chin. I could hear the noise of the women outside the door in the hallway. What if one of them came in?

I wondered what would happen if Tabitha saw me like this. I imagined the door opening slowly, quietly, as she slipped in and clinked it shut behind her. I saw that predatory smirk but this time it was laced with something else, want. Hunger. I'd stand in the tub to demand my privacy, admonish her for interrupting me. She'd see me standing there, the water dripping down my curves, my red hair unfurled and heavy against my skin. I would be flushed with indignation instead of embarrassment.

She'd take a step forward and run her fingers through the bright red curls, tightening them in her fist before giving a gentle tug. "A pity you hide these under that hat," she'd whisper before her eyes flicked up to mine. My hand moved along my face, mirroring the action of her fingers as her other hand slipped over my jaw to my lips, pressing down on the bottom one.

"How I've wanted you alone like this," she'd whisper. Her other hand fisted my hair, pulling a little harder, forcing me down to my knees in the tub. She released me then to pull her clothes off. I knew she was wearing finery—corsets or other such contraptions that took a partner to remove appropriately. Not today, in this dream of mine, they practically melted off her, exposing her naked flesh.

She was exactly as I'd pictured her in my mind time and time again. Long, lean with her honey gold hair unbound. Her green eyes swallowed me whole as they appraised me. Her breasts smaller, her nipples a darker pink that looked almost brown. The fine freckles on her nose painted her shoulder, down along her side like little bits of dust. I leaned forward to lick them, to see if they were real, if my kisses would smudge them off. She groaned and I pulled back to see they were still there. Real life roadmaps of where I wanted to explore.

She didn't say anything as her hand fisted the back of my hair, grabbing one of the knots to pull my neck back. I cried out as she forced me down further into the tub, aligning herself with my line of vision. She lifted a foot to place on the edge of the tub as she opened herself to me.

"This is what you've wanted, isn't it?" she breathed at last, her grip a vice on my hair. The pain of it sent a thrill down my body as my own hand grabbed at it, tugging until I was sure the hair was ripping from my head. I wanted to leave these hairs everywhere, long bits of red yarn for her to find on her body and immediately remember me.

"Yes," I breathed. It didn't take any convincing to bring my mouth to her pussy, reaching out tentatively to feel it. I imagined it was like mine, my hand tracing my own, feeling the puffy outer lips that parted with the lightest touch to expose what lay between. I splayed my fingers over her hip bones as I drew her to me. My tongue darted out to part her flesh more, exploring the length of her from her throbbing clit to her opening. My fingers moved from her hip to that opening, dipping in a finger and curling it as my tongue went back to her clit to flick and lick it. It drew short gasps from her every time I made contact with it, pushing against the exposed flesh. My other arm wrapped around her waist to pull her tighter to me so I could close the ridiculous distance still between us.

I added another finger as her knees weakened and she leaned harder into me, curling my fingers against the soft pad of flesh I felt inside. She was clamping on me now, tightening on my fingers to try to work them like I was working her. I closed my mouth on her clit, alternating sucking and licking the bud until she shuddered in my arm. I opened my eyes and gazed up at her. Her jaw slack, her eyes glazed as I watched her —looked into those beautiful green eyes—as I drove her to orgasm with my mouth.

I had to bite the flesh of my free hand, the one not between my legs, to keep the sound of my orgasm concealed from the woman I dreamed about just outside the door.

I toweled off and dressed myself in a fine robe they laid out for me. Shortly after, they went to work with my hair, which hadn't seen a brush in more days than I could count. "You must buy a brush," Veronica hissed under her breath. She looked about to sweat under the labor of tearing through my knots. My skin flushed at the sensation, feeling so much like my dream from before.

After much tugging, they fashioned it into an intricate braid and knot to mirror the style of the day. They finished it off with one of Tabitha's outfits, which was painfully tight on me. She had delicate curves compared to my more pronounced ones. They had to let much of the binding out for me to fit into it. I was larger than all the women at the brothel despite my poverty. After Pa died, a meal was never guaranteed, so we ate what we could, when we could. They managed to cinch the dress on me and the end result was unrecognizable. I was far from beautiful, and not even pretty, but I looked like a respectable high society woman. The dress was only scandalous because there wasn't enough fabric to cover my ankles or wrists due to my height. I could easily have been one of the high society women on the hill if it weren't for the two women who flanked me now.

"Now you're set to be seen in public," Veronica said, standing back proudly.

Tabitha frowned, tapping her lower lip as she thought. "I thought the end result would be more profound," her frown turning to a pout. I could feel the color creeping into my cheeks at the insinuation. I knew I wasn't beautiful, there was no need to rub it in. And the fact that she found me particularly unattractive made my stomach plummet. I couldn't make eye contact with her so shortly after that dream I had, her cruelty wasn't helping.

"Don't be unkind," Veronica shot Tabitha a look that could wilt flowers. "You look like a real high society woman, Louisa. Once we find something to fit you better, you'll feel it too. Come," she extended her hand for me to take, helping me to stand from my seated position in front of the wide vanity mirror. "Your hair would pair just right with a deep hunter green. I can see it now in my mind and I know just the shop to visit for such a delicacy."

Chapter 10

LATER THAT NIGHT—MUCH later, after what felt like eons of shopping in Clarkdale—we'd changed into evening clothing and went out on the town. It was an experience alien to me, having never visited a restaurant, much less a saloon. Veronica insisted on it, Tabitha invited a few of the other girls out to a popular joint. It was just off the main drag and known for having a sensational singer named Ella Grace.

The walk to the saloon was electric as the other girls chatted excitedly between each other. They welcomed me with open enough arms, though I wasn't sure why. I was an outsider that had only been in their presence a mere few days. I suppose I *did* create the very concoction that allowed them to continue to work and earn money. None of them would be cast to the street as a single mother of a bastard child; their trust wasn't misplaced. If anyone found out about my side business, I would surely be hanged for murder. We both had something to lose, and that mutual secret allowed them to link their arms through mine and parade down the dusty street with me.

No one could mistake me for one of them, however. Even

with a well-fitting petticoat and clean hair, I lacked much of the grace and style they had. They were all beautiful in their very separate ways where I was not. Tabitha's sparse freckles were dainty, mine took over my face and sometimes coalesced into big patches. Veronica's curvy hips gave her a certain allure, whereas I had no waist to speak of. The woman at the clothing store spent some time on alterations to try to flatter my figure. It was a lost cause, but the end result was that I was merely presentable. I was a shadow behind the others.

In the saloon, that fact didn't change. Men flocked to the group of women who fell right into place in the din of the room. There was no music but the chatter of the crowd was loud enough to fill the space. The women with me laughed and carried on with the men near the bar, coercing drinks from them. At first, I was ignored, thrown into a shadowy corner of the bar, sitting carefully on a stool. I felt awkward and uncomfortable as I prayed no one would approach me. No one harassed me, no one tried to shove a drink into my hand like they did with the other women. I could perch silently and observe the chaos around me.

"Louisa, have you ever had a spirit before?" asked Tabitha, leaning off the lap of a piss drunk miner. She extended her arm and handed me the drink she'd been sipping on, nearly sloshing the contents of it on her new found beau.

"No," I allowed.

"Come along, then, have a sip. You may find it exciting!" she winked then, those deep green eyes holding mine for moments longer than they ever had before. I felt that familiar sensation of butterflies in my stomach, threatening to rise to my throat and escape. I took the glass from her and held it to my mouth, trying not to smell the drink. It wasn't as foul as I anticipated, so I took a large sip as quickly as I could.

The sensation of burning sent me into a sputtering cough that made the group break into fits of laughter. "You're alright, Louisa!" Tabitha sang, reaching out to stroke my arm. I could still feel the whisper of her touch long after she pulled her arm away and went back to courting the man beneath her. It wasn't long before they left, probably back to the brothel.

"Have you no beau?" I asked Veronica, who hung around despite the small group breaking apart. Her and Celeste, a busty woman with red-blonde hair, were all that remained.

Veronica laughed, "I have many, but tonight I'm here for her." She extended a hand and pointed to the woman on the low stage. She was extraordinarily beautiful with raven black hair that fell to her waist in a wavy blanket, so against the fashion of the time with its tight knots. Her dress was equally foreign, loose and exposing a bit of neckline, a bit of shoulder, her ankles. It didn't look immodest like the outfits worn inside the walls of the brothel. I recognized it from my first day in Clarkdale with the Mexican cook and her flowing skirts and dresses so unlike anything I'd seen before. Ella Grace was her name, and she had the same dark skin tone of the Mexicans I'd seen around Jerome and the same wide face and bright, large eyes. She was older than I was, perhaps in her late 20's, and all smiles as she nodded to the band members around her. They were an assortment of miners, still dressed in their mining clothes, resting heavy instruments against them in the indoor light.

No introduction was needed. The moment she sat down and nodded to her band the rest of the saloon quieted immediately. It sent a shiver up my spine. She tapped her foot and said, just loud enough for her band to hear, "One...two...one two three, go!" They broke into a song then and the crowd suddenly burst into movement. "Why did love have to hit me like that? Why did love crawl under my skin like that? How did you break me boy, oh how did you do it?" Ella Grace had a voice that was smoky and smooth, with the hint of the accent I'd come to recognize amongst the Mexicans. Her voice was surprisingly low for a woman, but it was beautiful and inspired the entire crowd to jump up and move. Veronica tilted her head back and laughed, grabbing my arms and forcing me off the stool I hadn't moved from all night.

"Louisa, it's about time you had some fun!" she cried. Celeste wasn't far behind, circling me, tossing me between them until I found some semblance of dancing.

In Kansas, we had dances on occasion, though mostly associated with the school. Heather went to a few, and I had gone to one before becoming a permanent chaperone, but parties weren't something we spent too much time attending. Since moving to Jerome, the parties were far away memories. Even living above the general store and hearing the ruckus from Spooky's Lounge down the street on a weekend night was as close as I'd come to a party. We hadn't the time or resources, much less the connections, to be invited or welcomed. Until recently, we hadn't even had spending money.

I tried not to think of Heather then, falling into the reckless dancing with the other women. We danced for the remainder of the night until Ella Grace had sung her last song and the saloon threatened to close up for the night. They flashed their lights—a strange new electricity that I'd seen only in the train stations before moving to Jerome—signaling the saloon to clear out. It was just for show, they'd be closed no more than three hours for full cleaning before re-opening early in the morning to serve food and more alcohol to the miners who came off the overnight shift. Jerome might occasionally rest its eyes but it never truly slept.

Veronica twirled, drunk and happy, in the busy street in front of the saloon. It was packed with other groups spilling out of other saloons as they closed for the early morning hours, mingling together in their drunk reverie. "You've an admirer," Veronica whispered into my ear, nodding to a tall man standing off to the side of the building. He was well dressed, a smart looking man, with an imposing mustache and tall top hat. He was watching us closely and I quickly averted my gaze to Veronica.

"Don't be cruel, he's watching you and Celeste."

She laughed and twirled some more, shaking her head. "He's had an eye out for you all night." Her twirling continued down the street as she headed to Main Street and I split off to trek up the hill to my empty house.

The silence of the house was deafening compared to the loud ruckus of the saloon that assaulted my ears all night. The cabin suddenly felt large and empty, much too large for a single woman who spent most of her time at work. I considered my options then, staring at the bare walls and the empty kitchen. Decision made, I shed my strange new clothes for the comfort of my bedclothes and retired to bed.

Within a week I had sold the now too spacious cabin on the hill and moved my scant belongings into the brothel. Well, not exactly the brothel; a housing situation less than 10 feet away from the brothel where most of the women lived. Some did their business out of their own room in the brothel while others lived next door in this boarding house specifically for the women. It served as a halfway house for women in those in between situations as well, so a transient population came and went on the bottom floor.

My living quarters were comfortable. As I set about my last possession, I thought about the vast changes in housing I'd experienced in the last year. First a train, then a boarding house, then a house, then above a general store, then on the hill...now in a group housing situation with sex workers. The room was modestly sized, with my own personal toilet and bathing room. This place also had adequate plumbing to allow me to bathe without going to the well and I could enjoy more of those long, warm baths. The walls were decorated with wallpaper that felt homey and pleasant. Meals were prepared in the kitchen downstairs by the staff, which was ideal for me given my lack of true culinary skills.

Hiding my finances became a more important task now. I didn't trust the other girls (or maids or cooks or Jennie) not to trespass and rifle through my things, so I set up a few places with my money. The bank in Clarkdale, another bank in town if I needed fast cash, various hiding places in the garden, and always a small sum on my person. I'd learned enough sewing from Heather to create a hidden pocket within my petticoat to allow the storage of enough cash if I needed it for any reason. It required fully disrobing so I didn't run the risk of it falling out or being noticed accidentally. For once, my fleshy body came at an advantage.

I'd fallen into swing with my work to the point where I was quick and efficient and didn't nearly spend all day in the office going through old paperwork.

Tabitha came down with a cold two days after our outing at the saloon and took to rales and wheezes that kept the house up. After one night of fitful sleep, I consulted Ma's book and created an elixir for coughs and sore throats. I banged on her door at 2am one morning and handed her the jar wordlessly, before stomping away and returning to bed. The next evening, Tabitha was seen at dinner, looking nearly healed. Word spread and now the girls approached me for every minor inconvenience in their life.

"Do you have anything to help with love?" asked Celeste one day at lunch. I'd taken to sitting with Celeste and Veronica at lunch. I didn't find them particularly interesting or fun, but their presence was a welcome distraction from my own solitude. Tending to my garden and going through my paperwork offered a reprieve but, overall, I was bored and lonely. I missed Heather terribly but didn't even know where to look for her, much less if she were alive and doing well.

"What sort of potion would I have for love?" I asked. She shrugged, her utensil swirling the food on her plate slowly as she considered her words.

"You've got one for every other ailment, why not love?" Veronica set her own utensil down and looked at me intently, as though it was a question she'd been considering as well.

"Love isn't an ailment, it's not something to medicate," then, after seeing their distraught faces, I laughed. "Do you mean to tell me you've thought I dealt in magic this whole time? My Ma was a nurse, she knew the medicinal uses of herbs and plants and placed them together for tinctures. There's no magic or...or...witchcraft in any of this! It is just using plants for their known purposes." I frowned then.

"But...they work so well," Celeste insisted. "You're meaning to tell me there ain't a single plant known for bringing love?"

I shook my head. "Love isn't something that can be measured. Do you want plants that will make you smell appeasing? That may bring about love. Do you want mixes to make you relaxed and social? I have those as well. But love...you can't capture love."

"Have you ever been in love?" Celeste asked then, her own frown bigger than my own. "Because if you had, you'd have a potion to get it back." I thought of golden brown hair and a soft upturned nose, or the smoky voice in the saloon with the long black hair and wondered if I did know of love. The ache in my stomach at both memories only confused me more.

"Don't be daft, Celeste, if Louisa had a potion for love do you think she'd be living with us whores?" Tabitha appeared almost as if she materialized, plopping into a chair very near to us. She was wearing her bedclothes still, a flowing material that exposed her bruised collarbones and just the hint of the side of her breast. I dragged my eyes away and to my plate. Veronica caught my eye then, something unreadable flashing across her face.

Celeste was pacified by this answer and sat back, lifting her utensils once more with her frown still in place. "If you come upon a potion to bring me love, I will pay high dollar for it." We ate in silence after that.

Chapter 11

MISS JENNIE REQUESTED my presence later that month to accompany her to a social gathering. She'd mentioned during our initial meeting that I might have to attend such a function at some point and time. It was the main impetus behind buying me such stylish clothes on those first few days, and supplying me with many more outfits since then. Now that the local store had my measurements, they sent me at least one piece a week, paid for and picked by Miss Jennie. She ordered Tabitha and Veronica to do my hair and makeup once more, mostly because neither had been touched since the saloon weeks prior. Jennie stated on more than one occasion that I was a representation of her, much like her girls were.

None of the other women joined us as we took a carriage up Cleopatra Hill to a mansion on the side of the hill. I'd never gone this far up the hill and the view was breathtaking. I'd come to associate the rich reds on the horizon with beauty and find the once harsh browns comforting. It was a contrast from the green of my childhood, but I'd grown into a true adult under the looming Mingus Mountain and Cleopatra Hill.

"You weren't born here, were ya?" asked Miss Jennie halfway up the hill.

I shook my head. "Kansas," I allowed after I noticed she was staring at me expectantly, clearly having forgotten our first meeting.

She whistled under her breath at that. "Quite some way for a wee girl to travel," she remarked. She wanted details and I wasn't sure if I wanted to give them to her. "And your sister," she pressed, "has she returned to Kansas?"

I thought about that for a long moment. Would Heather return to Kansas? She expressed her hatred of the school children she once loved here and left school for that reason. With her skills—and the amount of money she took from me—she could have easily traveled home to Kansas and moved in with an aunt or uncle or some other family member we rarely spoke to. "I suppose," I allowed, glad to see the wagon pull up to the mansion at long last.

The driver helped us down from the wagon and lead us to the door, which he knocked on. "Madam Jennie and Miss Louisa to call," he told the man who opened the door. He nodded and led us through the tall, expansive hallway to a seating room filled with other couples. There were women— some that I recognized, some that I didn't—and girls, plus some men loitering about the edges. The women were all dressed similarly to Miss Jennie and me. The man paused at the threshold and announced, "Madam Jennie and her business associate, Miss Louisa." I was painfully aware of the silence that followed as the eyes turned to us.

Amongst the women, I saw my garden neighbor, who frowned and narrowed her eyes, trying to decide if I were the very same Louisa that shared a border with her or not. Now decked in expensive clothes, washed and groomed to the latest fashion, it was no surprise she couldn't marry my image to the lost, dirty girl from all those weeks ago. It gave me great happiness to see that most of the eyes were locked on Miss Jennie and not on myself. Miss Jennie waved to a woman in the corner who suddenly looked rather afraid, and we crossed the room to take a seat at her table. Jennie commanded the group, her shoulders were back, her chin raised, her gaze sharp.

"Jennie!" the woman exclaimed, hesitation obvious in her voice. There was also a bit of fear of Jennie herself or of being seen with her; I was unsure. "Who's this..." the woman hesitated, possibly meaning to pay me a compliment until I got close enough.

"Ah, yes Natalie. This is Miss Louisa, she's my new manager and nurse. She oversees the finances and general health of the girls. She's a very skilled nurse. Come, Louisa, sit," she patted a chair next to her and I stiffly sat in it.

"A nurse?" the woman looked surprised, giving me a once over again. "She's awfully young."

"My Ma, God rest her soul, was a nurse. I've been her apprentice since a toddler," I said with a stiff smile. This appeased the lady and she crossed herself.

"I'm sorry about your mother. What sort of nursing do you do?"

I chanced a side glance at Miss Jennie, who sat back with a wicked smile on her face. "General health," I said dismissively. "Ma worked with a general practitioner and midwife in Kansas, so I have considerable skills on maintaining health. Occasional colds, other little inconveniences."

Miss Jennie laughed her loud laugh at that statement. "Yes, those little inconveniences. Let's quit the inquisition on poor Louisa, Natalie, and play a bit of gossip."

Natalie relaxed visibly at this and a spark burned in her

dark brown eyes. "You mean the business dealings of the mine? The new buyers?"

Miss Jennie nodded enthusiastically at this, and the woman launched into a long tirade about buying and selling of the mine. I didn't understand the fine details but I did understand the numbers. From the sound of it, the mine was pulling resources at a number previously unheard of and was set to become the highest producing mine of all time. I thought about my Pa down in those mines, his body perpetually aflame from the ever present fire. How much production fell on the back of other people? How much would they sell his grave for?

I guess it didn't differ too much from my position. I was killing unborn children for sex workers to make enough money to...to what? Go to nursing school? Move out of Jerome? I was just hoarding cash and sitting on it like a dragon and his clutch.

"Louisa, dear," came the voice of the plump woman who was my neighbor.

I turned my head to acknowledge her, looking up at her from under the fringe of the hat Tabitha had practically sutured to my head. "Yes?" I asked.

She was standing just a foot from me, a frown lightly resting on her face. "Come, join me for a game of Cinch at my table." I chanced a glance at Jennie, who waved her hand dismissively, and joined her at a table with another woman and a man. They introduced themselves with names I forgot almost the moment they were said to me.

"How long have you been business associates with Miss Jennie?" asked my neighbor, whose name I now remembered was Coraline, within minutes of dealing out the cards.

I'd played the game once or twice before and knew enough to stumble through without looking too out of practice. Cards were reserved for a time when I had free time back in Kansas more than a year ago. Coraline didn't even try to hide her itch for gossip, she visibly squirmed as I sorted through my cards and arranged them, stalling my reply. "I've been providing medical care for a few months now, but only recently did I start to handle her books," I said at long last.

The two others at the table were just as intent on my words as Coraline, barely paying attention to their cards. "Medical care?" Coraline asked, shifting her cards around absently. Her voice was shrill yet hushed, wanting to keep the bit of gossip to herself.

"Ma was a nurse," I said. "I picked up her trade from an early age." The lie felt easy now that I'd told it twice in such a short span. I wondered what other false truths I'd tell about myself and my association with Miss Jennie and her brothel.

"Oh, I see!" Coraline cried as if in relief, playing a few cards. The silence spread between us until the game was nearly over. Once or twice, the others tried idle chatter, talking about some person I'd never met before and never heard of. After a few attempts, they gave up all pretenses of trying to integrate me into their conversation. From then on, it became droll talk of the weather, of new buildings, and of me sitting in silence while playing Cinch.

I rather preferred it this way.

The game ended and shortly afterwards, a call was made for dinner. "May I accompany you?" came a male voice to my left. I turned, already partially out of my chair, to see a man I vaguely recognized. He was the man from the saloon some weeks ago, with his bushy mustache and silly top hat. Now, he had no top hat and exposed a nearly naked head, though I doubted from balding alone. He was not particularly handsome and in the evening light that filtered in from the windows, he looked severe. His nose was too long and too pointed, his eyebrows too thick and nearly connected in the middle, and his lips were far too puffy. I did not take his hand and finished standing, realizing then I was almost his exact height.

"To the dining room, then," he said, his voice brisk but with an edge of humor to it. I managed to glance at Coraline's shocked face from the corner of my eye, though I didn't know what sort of scandal I was inviting by placing a hand on his extended elbow. What could be worse than Madam Jennie, owner of debauchery, peddler of flesh? Did he own a brothel of men that whored themselves in a similar fashion? No, I realized, that would simply be a common boarding house. They would provide such a service for free.

"Abraham," he allowed after taking a full step away from the table of gawking jaws.

"Louisa," I returned. He nodded. "Ah, yes, I know exactly who you are. Madam Jennie's...business associate?" He lifted a single eyebrow, though with their connection in the middle of his forehead it could have arguably been both.

"Your tone implies something," I responded.

He *tsk tsk* his tongue, shaking his head gently. "I imply nothing. You are her business associate, are you not? Some sort of manager? In charge of her wide finances. That's quite a task for a relative stranger." I chose not to reply, watching him pull back a chair at the long, large table for me to seat myself in. I simply thanked him and tried not to act annoyed when he sat himself next to me. Across the table and further down, I saw Jennie sitting, encircled by a group of men. I watched as they basically fought for her attention, tripping over themselves to be seated near her.

"They're always like that," Abraham said to me after seating himself.

"To her, or to any eligible female?" I asked.

He chuckled. "Madam Jennie is not an eligible female; you know that as well as I do. No, these men are the desperate sort. Squandered their fortune somewhere, or their parental funds have expired. They've enough prestige to be invited to these soirees but not enough funds to truly fit in. See the wear of the gloves? They show their poor fortune too readily. They need a woman with funds to abuse. It is their ticket to the top without doing an ounce of hard work, except for courting a woman who deals in flesh."

"That is a brilliantly cruel assessment," I said, though truly impressed. "I take it you haven't befriended any of these men?"

He barked a bitter laugh, shaking his head. "On the contrary, they run amongst me in familiar company. I know them *too* well." He took a sip of the drink sitting in front of him, frowning at it.

"It seems poor taste to speak ill of your friends," I said, taking a sip of my own drink. It was some sort of spirit—a wine, I think, judging by its color—and so dry and harsh it made my mouth pucker.

"They are as much a friend to me as Coraline is a friend to you." I couldn't help but laugh at this, drawing the attention of a few others at the table. They stared outright.

"It seems we've attracted attention," Abraham whispered to me.

I shrugged, "I've felt the stares since I got here. It seems that associating yourself with Miss Jennie invites attention."

"And you don't enjoy it?" he asked. I shook my head.

"I rather prefer being ignored." I almost admitted I missed the anonymity of the grocery store but I'd never let that slip.

"Now?"

I waved to my outfit, my hair, my everything. "This is a

costume to remain unseen amongst the women here. I try to fit in to fade away."

He nodded, understanding. "Being ignored? What sort of obscurity did Jennie pluck you from?"

I instantly regretted saying as much as I had. "A figure of speech," I allowed, shrugging.

His knowing smile told me how little he believed me. "Yes, I have heard that before. The figure of speech about a girl with hair the color of roses and fire, forever ignored."

I had no reply to that, so I took another drink of the foul wine. "Oh, don't mistake me. I am teasing—cruelly so. I know exactly who you are. I own the general store you worked at. I own all the general stores, actually. And some of the saloons. Plus part of the mine. Most of the mine."

Ah, that explained the stares. "That's quite an ambitious collection," I remarked, unable to feign interest. Hearing him speak so cavalier about his accomplishments was embarrassing to hear and grating to try to appreciate. I liked him better when he was taunting the men across the table.

"You don't sound impressed," he said, upset. Thankfully, at that moment, the host—who I hadn't met yet—stood up and clinked his glass with a fork. He spoke briefly about welcoming us to his table, celebrating the wealth of Jerome, the success of the mine... I'd tuned him out after a few more sentences. My eyes searched longingly for the food to make an appearance if only to get the taste of the wine from my mouth and to get Abraham to stop talking.

The host finished his speech and the first course of the meal came out, allowing a silence to set over the table while everyone ate. Abraham was sullen next to me until the third course, when he said, "I am sorry if I have offended you. I am used to women being impressed and intrigued with my success. "

The thought of him trying to impress or intrigue me made me want to laugh, which was at odds of the gross sinking in my stomach. It wasn't the butterflies I got when Tabitha looked at me, or when I heard Ella Grace sing. It was more like the time when I ate something foul and spent the afternoon vomiting. It was unsettling.

"You should be proud of your success. It is admirable," I offered, picking at my food now. My appetite was long gone.

"You don't appear to admire it," he said.

"Not particularly," I allowed. "We never had riches growing up, and I didn't know riches until recently. It's an alien feeling." It wasn't a complete lie, I just didn't want to admit to myself how good it all felt.

Abraham put down his silverware and regarded me oddly. "Well, do you like the riches?"

I shrugged. "I like not living in a box above a general store. I like having the ability to choose my fortune. These are things only afforded to the rich."

"But what of the clothes? The drink?" he pressed. I shook my head.

"The clothes are suffocating, but a necessity. This drink tastes like dirt."

He let out a loud laugh, his head tilted back, snaring the table once more with their attention. Despite myself, I felt a smile creep at the corners of my mouth. "Louisa, never change a thing." He returned to eating, his sullen mood lifted.

The dinner finished not much longer afterwards and Miss Jennie came to collect me. She didn't say much to me until we were safely on the wagon and nearly down the hill. "I see you've met Abraham," she said, her voice flat; a trap. I chanced a sideways glance, but the moon was new and did little to illuminate her features. I'd never heard her use any tone other than her typical jovial one, as though she were about to let you in on the joke.

"I did," I ventured.

Silence.

"And did you enjoy his company?" she pressed.

"He is a braggart. It's no wonder he has no friends." A full three breaths passed before Miss Jennie let out the loudest cackle I'd ever heard, and haven't heard since. She was nearly winded, sputtering her laughter into her hands, holding her stomach as she rocked. The man driving the carriage turned back to give us imploring looks, then quickly turned his gaze back to the road. Miss Jennie in a fit of hysterics was something no one truly wanted to witness.

"I hope you held your tongue in front of him," she said at long last, wiping her eyes with the edges of her dress sleeves.

"More or less," I said, and she snorted. Her breathing finally calmed as we came in sight of the brothel. It was just as bright as any other night of the week, Sabbath be damned. No rest for the wicked, I supposed.

"Abraham is a rich man intent on spreading his fortune. He once came to court me, but quickly realized he was not a match for me. Much less of an appropriate height." The carriage slowed and she hopped out before the driver could come around to help her out. The driver frowned at her and she shooed him away. "Off with ya, I'm not some fragile lass, I can hop out a foot or two. Onward!" Her waving started the horses and I nearly fell from the carriage I was presently half way out of.

"It seemed like you had quite a few suitors," I ventured.

She lifted her shoulders in a dismissive way, looking up the hill to the expansive mansions above our heads. "I've one true love, Louisa, and it's power." Her eyes lowered on me and in the dim light of the porch of the boarding house I understood exactly what she meant: My nest egg of money, used for absolutely nothing. The power of it all, though.

"Entertainment," I offered, turning a last look to the brothel a few hundred yards away. "We need to hire entertainment."

"We?" Jennie asked.

"As your business associate, I suggest we hire singers as they do in the saloons. Even a piano player, something lively. Music and spirits downstairs, sin upstairs."

She regarded me silently, then said, "I'll consider it," before disappearing through the door to her office.

Chapter 12

WITHIN A WEEK, Jennie started converting the downstairs parlor to mirror a saloon, and within two weeks, we had a singer twice weekly and a piano player on odd days. More often than not, we had livelihood, music, dance. Jennie's place was no longer just a brothel, it was the CatHouse. It was the richest of all her brothels and all the star of Jerome.

The singers who came to entertain were just as decadent as Ella Grace. One particular singer came out of nowhere—a short girl with equally short blonde hair. Her voice was high pitched but melodic, so unlike the smoky drawl of the music of the time. Her twang was something that identified her as being from the east coast, "Bawston," she told me one night. Her name was Cassidy Rich and I was immediately in love.

The entertainment came to the brothel the night or day before their stint depending on how far they'd traveled, and stayed in a guest room in the neighboring boarding house. Cassidy traveled with three men, all relatives and bandmates. They insisted Cassidy stay near them, even though it would have been inappropriate for them to stay with the other women. The men stayed a few doors down while Cassidy took the guest room nearly adjacent to mine with access to my bathing room. Normally, I had the area to myself since guests rarely stayed in that particular room, but I didn't mind. Cassidy was beautiful and vibrant.

I gave her a tour of the facilities, both the brothel and the boarding house, giving her time to unpack her strange clothing and strange little suitcases. "This is my first time in Arizona," she confided in me. The way she said 'first' and 'Arizona' were so strange to me, I almost didn't recognize the words.

"Do you travel often?" I asked, desperate to hear her speak some more.

She nodded, unpacking her things into the standing armoire. "Quite often, this is the farthest gig. But we're riding out of the south these days, hoping to head to California. Hear it's the pot of gold and I'm after riches," she winked at me over her shoulder.

"Jerome has the richest mine in the world," I said, not realizing it was out of my mouth until too late. She paused, then turned slowly to look at me. "Now, how did you wander upon that figure?" Her eyebrow was quirked in a way that caused my stomach to flutter.

"I am a business woman. I make figures my livelihood."

She let out a low "hmm," then turned back to unpack her things.

Cassidy spent most of that day and the next with me. She insisted I show her around the town, investigating all the hideouts, the saloons, the people worth knowing. She found the township charming, despite the fact it was dirty and hot. She fanned herself and laughed merrily. "Where I'm from," she said, moving close enough that I could count every eyelash, "the air is humid. It's thick."

"I know of it," I told her, confiding that I was from Kansas, that I'd only moved here recently. I told her of Pa, of Ma, of Heather. She listened in rapt attention, marveling at how my life had changed so drastically.

"And now you find yourself the associate of someone like Miss Jennie?" she marveled, her fingers playing along the edges of my gloves. She was a great listener, only interrupting me to ask more questions. She wanted to know everything about me, and she spent all her free time with me.

Cassidy played two nights in a row with plans to stay another week or two to tour Jerome. The first night was busy, the second night was packed tighter than it ever had been before. It was no secret that Cassidy had a draw much like the sirens of childhood lore, singing in her high pitched voice about everything from love to ruckus.

"Son of a bitch! Pour me another!" she sang, stomping her foot to the beat of the cello her cousin strummed animatedly. I sat in my usual spot, far in the back of the room, nearly hidden by the curtains. It was elevated enough that I could keep an eye on the main floor and ensure nothing out of sorts was going on. Since we allowed entertainment in the front room, the workers wore more clothing here, shedding it as they disappeared deeper into the building. I had clear visual access to the bar and the staircase, as well as a line of vision to the hallway with the offices. Those were locked tight this time of night.

I sat in the window and watched her sing.

"She's quite good," came a voice from my side, and I jumped, angry at myself for being so oblivious. Abraham, I recognized, his hat pulled off and held absently in his hand. He was dressed better than the other men in the foyer, who all eyed him carefully. I wasn't sure if it was because they knew who he was or because they knew a well-dressed, rich man made for too much competition for the woman of their choice.

"Abraham, have you come to find yourself a woman?" I asked, avoiding his eye.

"I actually came for one woman in particular...well, two. You and Madam Jennie. I had to see what sort of ploys you two have to put me out of business." He smiled a mild mannered smile, but there was a hint of malice in the upturned corners of his mouth.

"Just a small remodel," I offered, wishing he'd leave so I could continue to watch Cassidy sing.

"A small remodel indeed," he said, frowning. "This seems like a lucrative venture." He was pressing, stepping closer to me, attempting to move me over with his closeness so he might sit next to me. Thankfully, I was wide enough to disallow such a thing, and I wasn't one to give up my perch to a man.

"I suppose," I offered, turning my head back to Cassidy. She looked at me from across the crowd and gave a quick wink, kicking up a heel as she launched into another high paced song.

"Would you care to dance?" he asked.

I shook my head. "I'm quite content to listen, I'm afraid I'm not much of a dancer."

"No one is much of a dancer," he agreed, grabbing my arm and pulling me to my feet against my will. I almost slapped him for his aggression when I caught the eye of Miss Jennie from across the bar. Something on her face, something I couldn't quite place—a silent pleading—told me to go ahead and dance with him. I allowed him to lead me across the floor, my mouth drawn into a tight line. I followed him wordlessly to the opening of the floor just as Cassidy kicked into a slower song.

"This one is for those love birds out there," she drawled. I felt my face turn shades of red and was thankful for the low lighting.

"What drove you two to come to such an idea as this?" he pressed after half a second on the floor. "Remodeling, that is," he added.

"Just a suggestion; I suppose she found it appealing." Another long silence ensued.

"So it was your idea?" he asked.

"Yes, modeled after the saloons. The two businesses aren't too different."

"No, they certainly are not," he agreed, his tone pensive. Silence stretched between us as we moved stiff and awkward to Cassidy's heartbreaking song. I listened to her intently, trying to pretend Abraham was not there. "...don't you think?" I caught the end of his statement, realizing how far I had distanced myself.

"I'm sorry, I'm afraid I didn't hear you," I apologized.

A half smile played on his lips. "Wherever did you find this singer? She's delectable." His tone was predatory.

"Miss Jennie works in mysterious ways." The song ended and I stepped away from him, giving a polite nod.

"Thank you for the dance," he said, adjusting his shirt. "I'm afraid I must be off. Send my regards to Madam Jennie, I shall call soon." He set his hat on his head once more and tipped the edge to me in farewell.

I enjoyed the rest of the night in solitude on my window bench, listening to Cassidy sing, undisturbed.

Cassidy continued to call on me every morning for a tour about Jerome, or just a walk, or even just a cup of tea. She preferred to be out of the boarding house and didn't really go near the other brothels. It was just her and I, wandering the streets, enjoying each other's company. She was quickly becoming a friend and more than once I caught her stealing glances at me. Her eyes would linger on my wrist if my sleeve rode up, or along my collar bone. Once, I tried to meet her eyes and she cast them downward quickly with a blush.

She wanted to know about the others, too. She was fascinated in the workings of the brothel and how much money it took in. How much went to the women? Did they get paid by the brothel, or did I collect from them? How much money did Jennie truly have?

I took her to the mine once and she held my hand as I looked upon the graveyard where my father still burned. We watched in silence before setting off back to the boarding house.

One night, Cassidy sat down next to me at dinner, interrupting my reading. I normally ate alone or with Celeste but she was working the afternoon and wouldn't be done until much later. "Will you be at Cathouse tonight?" she asked me.

I set down my book and nodded. "Yes, I rather enjoy the entertainment nights."

"Do you?" she asked, surprised. Her eyebrows were so expressive.

"You seem surprised," I said.

"You just don't seem like you much enjoy it."

If only she knew.

"Louisa is a real stick in the mud," said Tabitha, sitting down near us with a wicked smile on her face. All the months of living with her and I still felt the rush in my stomach when she spoke to me.

"There's nothing wrong with a woman with morals," Cassidy returned, her smile no longer amused. Now it was terse, a straight line directly across her face.

Tabitha started, "What do you know of morals? You're playing in a literal whore house. We peddle in the flesh here; you knew that when you landed this gig."

Cassidy shrugged. "I also know what I'm worth, and it's more than anyone here," she said, her voice not kind.

Tabitha stood up then, pushing her chair back loudly. "Well then, miss 'Bawston' Queen. I hope it's not too immoral of me to tell you to kindly fuck off." Tabitha took her tray of food and dumped it into Cassidy's lap then, destroying her snow white dress. The rest of the eating area was silent as Tabitha turned and strode out, her shoes making an echoing clack-clack as she exited. Cassidy sat in shock for a full minute before standing, letting the food slide off her lap and onto the floor.

"Come, let's get you cleaned up," I said, my voice calm despite the rush of blood in my ears. I was sure my face was the color of the beet sauce now staining her previously flawless white dress. "Manuel, please clean this up," I motioned to one of the workers as I led her up the stairs to our apartments. "You go ahead and get changed. I'll grab some cold water so we can soak it before it sets."

I went to grab some lemons and a bucket of cold water with every intention of meeting her in the guest room. I trudged to our bathing room then, surprised to see her standing nearly naked in the middle of it. I jumped, partially spilling the water bucket on the floor. "My apologies, Miss Cassidy, I thought..."

I stuttered, flailing to catch the lemons that I dropped in the process. The bucket of water landed with a thud and spilled bits of sudsy water over the edge. "I'll leave you be, uhm, yes..." I stammered, backing to the door with my gaze averted.

"Miss Louisa, are you shy?" she asked. She seemed unfazed by her nakedness and by my witnessing it. "Haven't you a sibling? Do you not live in a brothel?" she laughed, hands on her hips, exposing her more. "Why, your face is red as a lobster! Come, don't be so shy."

"It's immodest," I protested, a feint, still trying to back out the door without looking at her.

"Nudity is not immodest, not in the way the women here lack modesty. It's a sin to fornicate as they do for money. Nudity, sex, that's all natural. If you're in love," she added, taking a step toward me. "You're not like these other girls, are you?" she asked, reaching a hand out to place it on my covered arm. It was hot where she touched me, even through the fabric.

"I...I don't know what you're getting at." I wanted to pull my arm away but I couldn't muster the strength. Her grip closed on my arm, refusing to let me go if I tried to slink away.

"These other girls—vile and simple. They can't think beyond tomorrow. You're intelligent, you're...different." My eyes slowly rose to meet her own, the deep blue that had become so familiar over the last few days. Her grip tightened on that arm as she pulled me forward, putty in her hands. I was painfully aware of how little distance was between the two of us, how her soft exposed curves weren't far from my painfully clothed ones.

"I..." I still couldn't find the words to say, the words she wanted. She smiled then, her eyes half lidded, and she leaned in to press her soft lips against my own. I didn't dare move a muscle, letting the sensation of her lips wash over me. My heart was hammering loud enough in my chest, I was sure the entire house could hear if they'd only listen. Her fingers traced their way up my arm to my face, pulling me closer when I didn't respond, probing my jaw until I kissed her back.

A kiss.

Before I knew it, my own hands were in her short hair and I was pulling her into me too, feeling a release of an ache in my chest I hadn't felt before. The tension of the last year broke from my center, from my body, and I went from putty in her hands to a flame that needed to be fed. Cassidy was kindling.

If she was put off by my sudden advance, by my sloppy and unrefined kissing, she made no mention. I'd watched the girls work enough to get the gist of it, I hoped that she understood enough to lead me.

She lead my fingers from her hair to her exposed breasts, allowing me to feel the weight in my hands, the softness of her skin that was so different from my own. She released my hands, moving instead to the buttons along the neck of my dress. One by one, she released them, exposing my freckled throat, which she met with her mouth. Her other hand reached for my bonnet and untied it, letting my hair tumble down and over my shoulders. She leaned back then, her eyes heavy lidded as she watched those curls fall over my face. Her fingers slid through them, "I knew you weren't like the others," she whispered.

Her mouth was on mine again, then along my jaw to my ear to whisper, "Turn around." I did, slowly, as if in a trance, feeling her fingers slide under the various ties and buttons of my dress, working it off slowly, methodically. As it slipped down my shoulder, her mouth met my exposed flesh, kissing each freckle slowly. I'd scarcely been able to breathe, afraid that if I did, she'd blow away in smoke and mist.

My dress slid off my shoulder and down around my waist. She turned me back around then, appraising me. I was a full head and a half taller, making it easy for her to make those kisses journey down along my chest and my breast. I inhaled sharply as her mouth closed over a nipple, feeling a heat so foreign but so welcome explode across my stomach. I was sure if I looked in the mirror I would see that my face was the color of my hair but I didn't care. I didn't want her to stop.

"Have you ever done this before?" she asked, releasing my hard nipple from her teeth with a devious grin up at me. I shook my head, letting out the breath I was holding. She was still there, staring at me with those blue eyes, her face unreadable.

No, not unreadable. I'd seen that look on my own face before. It was hunger.

"Let me show you, then," she said. Her hands went to my hips and helped my dress the rest of the way down. I felt a flush at my sudden nakedness, large where she was small. My hands went to cover my breasts, my pussy, anything that was exposed. She only tsked and retrieved one of my hands from covering me, pulling me with gentle tugs to my bedroom. "Come," she said. "Let me show you what you've been missing."

She shut the door to the bathing room, leaving both our clothes in a pile on the floor. I cast one last look over my shoulder before stepping into my room. She looked over it with one quick glance before resting her eyes on my bed. She released my hand enough to sit me on the edge of my bed. Cassidy knelt in front of me, gently prying my thighs apart as she situated herself between them. She looked up at me with those piercing eyes. "Is this what you want, Louisa?" she asked. Her voice was heavy, that hungry look back in her eyes. The way she said my name...it elicited something wild in me, I couldn't speak. I just nodded. "You cannot just nod; you must say it. Tell me, 'Yes, Cassidy, I want this. I want *you*.'"

My throat was dry, probably because my jaw had been slack, but I managed out a fumbling reply, "Yes...Cassidy. I want...I want this. I want..." the heat was creeping up my shoulders, then down to between my thighs. "I want you."

With that, Cassidy lowered her mouth to my right ankle, curling her fingers around it as she kissed and licked and bit slowly up my inner thigh. The higher she went, the more intense the sensations became, running like lightning from that sensitive, soft skin to the area between my thighs. This was nothing like my imagination, nothing like all those nights I spent watching and touching myself. This was better than anything I could have conjured on my own.

When her mouth reached the delicate flesh between my legs, it knew exactly where to kiss, how to slide her tongue to open me wide. I groaned loudly, too loudly, biting my lip to stifle the noise as her fingers followed her mouth. My thighs relaxed, no longer clenched against her. She placed one finger slowly inside of me and it was the most strange, most lovely sensation. I was content to feel her finger sliding in and out of me, slick with my wetness. My head lolled back and my eyes closed, my hips lifting off the edge of the bed.

That's when her mouth lowered again and it closed on my clit, bringing a sensation that was overwhelming and euphoric. I suppressed a squeal as her mouth closed over the area and licked and sucked. She continued to circle it slowly, languidly, while she added a second and third finger. Before I knew it, the area became so sensitive, a thick heat building under my hips that threatened to spill out.

She must have known too, her mouth became hungry and

probing, digging deep into my very being, matching my movements as I writhed and bucked under her.

The sensation came to a head and an overpowering feeling of elation filled my body, filled my bones. My toes curled, my head tilted even further backward, my mouth opened in a wordless prayer of ecstasy. My sweat slick thighs stopped moving, instead clamping against her, her mouth, her hands. I felt the vibrations of her moan against me, causing another delighted wave to crash over me. She slowed, her hands sliding along my thighs, my abdomen, waiting until I'd fully relaxed.

I looked down at her, looking down at the most beautiful woman I'd ever seen in my entire life.

She smiled up at me, her face glossy with my wetness. She used the back of her hand to wipe her face.

"Show me how you like it," I said to her, breathless. She grinned a devious smile in reply.

Chapter 13

SHE LEFT A WEEK LATER.

I felt the void of her absence in a way I'd never felt before. Not when Ma or Pa died, not when Heather left, not when we left Kansas. I knew there was no use convincing her not to leave. She'd told me on that first day that she wanted to go to California. Arizona was a stepping stone, and with the money she collected from her short two week gig, she had more than enough to head to California with her cousins.

The last night, while we lay in bed together—her head resting on my chest, our fingers entwined—she promised she'd return to me. "Louisa, you know I can't leave you for long," she sighed happily. I felt my heart race like it had the first day, the first time. That sensation didn't ebb; it was like every time was the first time.

"I swear to you, I'll return once I have the funds. We need a set up, we need to get started. All the promise of music and picture shows is in California. Once we get our roots, once we have it goin', I'll come back. Before that, even, we'll play shows..." we silenced each other with kisses and comforted each other with touch.

"You don't need money. I have money," I told her. I'd told her it time and time again: I had money, lots of money, squirreled away for an education or an adventure that never seemed to come. She relented and took a little, just enough to get to California, but not enough to stay. I would give her anything she asked for—money for her ticket, for food, for housing once she got there. The thought of her suffering pained me.

The entire week after she left was nothing but rain, turning the clay streets into a swamp. The new singers and entertainers moved into her room, creating a void of where she once was. They unpacked their things and left swirls of foreign energy, putting their suitcases on the floor we lay on together, talking into all hours of the night. By candlelight I showed her Ma's journal, told her about Heather and Pa and the general store. We laughed about Abraham. She told me about her childhood in Boston, taught me words in German, showed me how to strum a guitar.

The rain was a pathetic fallacy, truly, because I felt like a walking storm cloud.

Breakfast two days after she left had no respite from the endless rain. I sat alone at my table, chewing my breakfast silently, until Tabitha sat across from me. I hadn't seen her in nearly a week and her presence surprised me. "Someone's looking stormy," she commented brightly. "Is it because your little moral compass is gone?"

"What do you want, Tabitha?" I asked.

"Oh, nothing, just checking to see how you're doing. Are you alright now that you've got to spend your time with us whores? Us immoral hussies?" She laughed, tossing her golden brown hair over her shoulder. I frowned at her upturned pig nose and too close together eyes.

"Tabitha, don't be unkind," said Celeste, shot at her from across the table. She'd joined me some minutes prior but hadn't said a word to me.

"I'm just asking!" Tabitha replied, feigning innocence. "I wanted to know if our Louisa missed the Virgin Mary, and if she would lower herself to be seen with us once more."

"You know I don't think lowly of you despite your circumstances," I said with a sigh, putting my utensil down. My appetite, already finicky, was suddenly gone.

"Despite my circumstances, hmmm, I bet not. It's not as though we existed to you just a few days ago. Too busy with that Boston charlatan," she pressed.

I shrugged. "It's common courtesy to show a guest around and be hospitable. You are all too busy working, it seemed poor taste to leave her to her own devices."

"And her cousins? Did you test their devices too?" There was something malicious in her voice when she said it, her eyebrow raised accusatorially at me. "Ya didn't seem to do much leaving the building, if you ask me."

I felt the red rising to my face then, always such an obvious creature. It's a wonder I could keep a single secret. "What are you trying to say, Tabitha? Out with it already, I haven't the time for your games."

She was placated by that, though only momentarily. I couldn't decide if she was hesitant to say what she was thinking or she truly didn't believe I'd demand it of her. "I just want to know what you're scheming with a pretty girl from the east, that's all."

"Yeah, Tabitha, what are you trying to accuse Miss Louisa of?" pried Celeste, leaning over her food to look Tabitha in the eye. "Of conspiring to become a musician? Of having unsavory dealings with the lots of them?"

Tabitha set her mouth in a firm line and shook her head. "I was just jesting. You need to lighten up. All of you." With that, she grabbed her tray and rose, turning to give me a final look over her shoulder. While her look wasn't unkind it was obvious it was a warning.

Three days passed and the rain finally stopped, drying the ground up to something firmer and less like slush. The days were getting shorter and cooler, a welcome break from the oppressive heat of the Arizona summer. Cassidy told me in Phoenix, a city just a few hours south of us, the temperatures reached over 100 degrees. The thought perplexed me, I found Jerome to be hot enough in the summer to be almost unbearable.

On that third day, five days after Cassidy left, I heard a knock on my door to my office. "Yes?" I asked, looking up from my stack of paperwork. It'd been ignored entirely when Cassidy was here and now it overflowed.

"Miss," said the sweeper boy in his broken English. "Man here for you," he nodded at me. I stood and went to the parlor, where Abraham stood. He looked uncomfortable in his incredibly dressed down outfit, flicking incessantly at his wrists where cuffs should have been.

"Ah, Miss Louisa," he said, his smile breaking across his face in a wide, sweeping movement.

"Hello Abraham," I said, not returning his formalities. "Is there something I can help you with?" I asked.

"Oh, no, I've come to call, just as I said I would. I

wondered if you'd take the afternoon off to hike with me?"

"Hike?" I questioned. The little I knew about Abraham told me this was not an activity he routinely participated in, much less enjoyed.

"Yes," he agreed stiffly. "Nothing too strenuous, I'm afraid I'm not in any sort of shape for that. Just a little jaunt, shouldn't take more than a few hours." He extended his hand, which held a version of the hat he always wore, to the windows. "It's much too nice a day to stay inside."

"What a lovely proposal," Miss Jennie said, leaning on the door frame from the hallway to the offices. How she knew he was there I'll never know, but little went on that Jennie didn't notice. "What a wonderful way to relieve your melancholy, Louisa. The sun is the oldest cure. As a nurse, I'm sure you knew that." Her smile slowly spread across her face as she spoke.

"Melancholy? What ails you?" Abraham inquired.

"It is nothing—the rain, as she said. Yes, I will join this... hike...with you. Let me collect something more appropriate to wear. Have a seat."

Miss Jennie followed close behind me, announcing, "Let me help you. I have just the hat for the sun." She was silent until we'd entered the boarding house and climbed the steps to my room. She closed the door and locked it, turning to look at me. "I must ask something of you," she said. I sucked in a breath, knowing this would happen sooner or later.

"Yes?" I questioned, trying to keep calm.

"You must allow Abraham to court you. Well, falsely court you. He has every intention of taking over my brothels, or expanding his own. He's tried before in the past and did not succeed. It turns out that women would rather work for another woman than a man." She smiled at this, knowingly. I released a breath in relief. She was here to talk about Abraham, not Cassidy. "I suspect he's taken a keen interest in you for your connection with me."

"He's got no interest in me," I retorted.

"You are so new to this, Louisa, I'm afraid you don't understand the politics of the elite of Jerome. I have seen Abraham chased by every eligible woman in the Verde Valley. He finds some mortal flaw with them almost upon meeting. He's never called upon a woman before, not in my memory or anyone else's. Did he not come see you last week? It is suspect that he's latched onto you, of all people, so readily."

"Is it suspect?" I asked, taken aback.

"What, do you think he fancies you? Louisa, you are a woman with a business mind that is much like my own. Our strength is not our beauty or charms, as neither of us possess them. Our strength is business." I did not argue, though I did not entirely believe it as truth. Cassidy thought I was beautiful. She would spread my red hair out on the bed and run her fingers through it until there wasn't a single knot. She would kiss every freckle, one by one. She told me, time and time again, how charming she found me. I didn't need some man, much less Madam Jennie, trying to take that from me.

"What would you have me do, then?" I asked, clenching my jaw to keep from cursing her.

"You're a clever girl. Lie to him, give him half-truths, do whatever it is you do to be evasive. No one here knows a single thing about you except the lies you tell them. It shouldn't be too difficult to concoct some more to get him to divulge his business plans. He's interested in the mine but I want to get on it first. There's a lot of money to be made in that pit. They say it's pulling more than they ever thought it could." She smiled dreamily at this prospect.

Oh. So that's what this was about. "I don't tell any lies," I retorted by way of evasion. She didn't bother to acknowledge my words.

She rifled through my things before handing me a blouse with skirt, a simple outfit to pair with his dressed down attire. It would fair well for the tame fall day and if it got dirty it wasn't too much of a loss. Jennie nodded to herself, exiting. Before she was fully gone, she turned to look at me pointedly, "It benefits us both if we can sneak this mine out from under him. Remember that."

Abraham was waiting outside the brothel, looking just as uncomfortable as he looked inside. I'm sure it frustrated a man of his stature to be seen—wearing what he was wearing—outside of a brothel in the middle of broad daylight. Yes, Jerome was a 24-hour town, but those who frequented the brothel during the day were notoriously foul creatures. I'd seen them, drunk in broad daylight, detaching themselves from holding up the walls to try to buy women for less than the cost of a drink. Madam Jennie's establishments were expensive and high quality. The women were attractive and, with my help, never out of service for pregnancy. Scourges were not welcomed.

When Abraham saw me, he sighed in obvious relief. Whether it was for my equally dressed down attire or because he wasn't entirely sure I would show, I did not know. He extended his arm to allow mine to join his, and we set off the short distance in the direction of Mingus Mountain.

Calling what we did a "hike" would be hyperbolic. The trail was flat with a very gradual slope and took us to a most pedestrian overlook of the Verde Valley and the city below. We rested then on a rock most likely placed there for sitting, relaxing after our brief excursion. Abraham was considerably winded from the adventure, which was a shock given how light of frame he was. I was easily twice his weight and showed no outward signs of fatigue, which bothered him quite a bit. "Recovering from a cold, you see, that's why this is so taxing for me," he explained.

I shrugged. "It's quite the feat of fitness, this mountain," I offered, trying to hide the bite from my words. He didn't seem too amused by my comment, though, and fell into sullen silence. "How much of this do you own?" I asked, unsure how else to broach the subject.

He lit up immediately, rising from his sad stupor. "Ah, yes, well...if you trace the edges of the hill down, you'll find the Daisy Mine; I own most of that. A few small shares are for sale, but I intend on buying those in a month's time. I just need to move some finances around, appeal to a few investors. In due time. Otherwise, look to Main Street. Most of the saloons I own, and the restaurant and general store on the edge. I've considered moving into Hull Avenue...but I haven't decided yet." He suddenly stopped his discussion, a critical eye turned to me. "Why do you inquire?"

"Curious, I suppose. How a man with a saloon becomes a man with a mine. I don't imagine the two worlds collide very often."

He laughed, patting my knee reassuringly. "Oh, my dear, they do! Property is property. A man is known for his investments, and owning a mine is no different than owning any other bit of property. Think of this: You buy a plot and then you farm it. You buy a spot of land and you build on it. You buy a mine, you mine it. It's all the same, really, it's just certain talents are required." His tone was condescending, as though I did not singlehandedly double the income of Madam Jennie's in a few months' time.

"And you've talents to help with the saloons? And the mines?" I pressed.

He nodded. "Oh, yes, indeed. You've never met Mister Sherman, my business partner, but he oversees most of the saloons. He's the manager and decides the more mundane business transactions. I have others here and there, and then of course I have an associate I consult on all my mine business."

"And you believe purchasing the whole mine would be a smart decision?" I asked.

He nodded. "Very much so. Louisa, can you keep a secret?" His voice had quieted, and he looked either way as he said it.

"Who have I to tell my secrets to? The whores?" I asked, feeling the words burn on my tongue. It wasn't a word I used often and it felt heavy and noxious.

"Miss Louisa!" he said, after a shocked laugh. "I don't expect that you spend too much time associating with them, correct? Just out of necessity?" His tone was imploring, suggesting something I disliked.

I shrugged. "It's important that they trust me so I can deliver the upmost medical care. Truly, though, I don't call any of them my friends."

"You and I have that in common, then. Lots of associates, no friends. Perhaps we can become friends?"

I doubted that. "Perhaps. It is nice to take a break from business and just talk to someone. A welcome distraction, really."

He considered this for a moment, then nodded. "Yes, a break from business. Yet, here we are, talking about our respective businesses. I'm sure Madam Jennie's is booming?" I knew this was my opportunity to do as Madam Jennie instructed. If business booms, we both boom.

"Can you keep a secret?" I asked him, parroting his previous tone.

He smiled in that conspiratorial way. "I suppose a secret for a secret is a fair trade. As a business woman you can agree?"

I nodded, then looked away, trying to form the appropriate words. "Business isn't as swell as it would seem. The singers fees are high, and the remodel wasn't a cheap task. Jennie's been suffering for a while; it's why she fired the last girl and got me. I haven't been paid in quite some time. She actually wanted me to seduce you, to try to marry into a rich family to help with finances. She wants to remodel the entire line of brothels to look like Cathouse, even with the steep singer fees." I let the silence stretch between us as he processed that, trying to decide if I'd made the right move or not.

"I knew it!" he exclaimed at long last, pumping his arm overhead in joy. "I knew it! I knew that woman wasn't all the business she claimed to be! Ha!"

"Your turn," I said, after the silence stretched beyond what I found bearable.

"I'm not sure I should tell you now," he said, a ghost of a smile on his lips. "I'm afraid you'll poach me for my funds."

I laughed, shaking my head. "Don't you worry, Mr. Abraham, I am my own woman and make my own choices."

He smiled at this too, leaning a bit closer. "I don't believe I've heard you truly laugh before," he said softly.

"You're being evasive intentionally and I won't stand for it," I replied.

"Ah, yes...well. The mine. You see, these shares are quite important to me because of what was found just a week ago. The shares went up for sale because the general strength of the mine is lacking. It's producing a decent amount, but investors are losing hope for the serious boom that it should bring. That it was promised to bring. Just last week, we stumbled upon a hidden vein that promises to boast wealth of unknown proportions for years to come. We're sitting on a literal and figurative gold mine that will make Jerome the richest city in the west, if not the country. They're not profitable because they lack the infrastructure to harness them. There are shares in the east and the west, the west are the ones I'm banking on." He stopped there, sitting back, a wide smile breaking across his face.

"That's it?" I asked, using every ounce of restraint to keep calm and collected. He looked rather shocked by my nonchalance.

"That's it?!" he echoed, his voice high, those thick eyebrows nearly overlapping in the middle of his head. "Everyone already knows the Jerome mine is profitable..."

"Everyone thinks the Jerome mine is profitable, yes, but in danger of drying up and underproducing. Investors haven't touched this place in nearly a decade, and they're heading out to California in striking numbers—gold is worth more than copper. It's only a matter of time, Louisa, before our money well runs dry. Everyone here is supposed to think the mine is profitable. If they thought otherwise, they'd leave and we'd have no workforce. We'd become a ghost town, sitting on a failed mine. Investors come, inspect the numbers and leave. We need this, this push, to bring us to the forefront. If I go public with this information too soon then I'll never purchase the shares necessary to obtain the appropriate wealth. It's a balancing act, because if I wait too long there will be no investors, or the information will leak on its own." He paused here, eyeing me with scrutiny. "You don't plan to go public with this?"

I laughed again, though this a dry and humorless laugh. Public? No. "I'll try not to use my social graces and immense friend group to spoil your secret," I allowed. He laughed at this too, not minding that I didn't answer his question.

"And what of the miners? Do they get compensated for this new find?" I asked. He shrugged, pulling out a pocket watch to check the time. "Perhaps we can lower work hours to eight a day, maybe lower the days worked to five. But we'll need to hire more to make up for the gaps, and we can afford it."

"You must do something. They'll be unwilling to work for no improved compensation. They're not daft, they'll notice if they're pulling more out than previously." He nodded at this, tapping his chin. "And what about their families? Do you compensate the families of the men who die in the mine?"

"Die?" he asked, incredulous. "Families? Whatever do you mean?" I shook my head, trying to dismiss it.

"An innocent question," I said.

"No, no, you never have innocent questions Louisa. Death in the mines, what is this?"

"I just mean that I've seen the fires in the mine that can't be put out. Men die in those; you can't deny that. And if the fire isn't put out, then the family will never have a body to bury. That family just lost their sole source of income. I wanted to know if there were any compensation for those families."

He watched me carefully and I hoped he wasn't reading right through me, somehow finding the information about my Pa and his death written on my face. He knew I worked at the general store because he owned it. But he owned the mine, too, and my Pa had worked there. I tried to tell myself I was being paranoid, but I couldn't help it. "I never considered that. It would do quite something for morale, wouldn't it? To compensate those families for at least a few months to let them acclimate to a new life? Hmm, curious. I wasn't even truly aware of these fires. You say they burn forever?"

"Yes, I've been told they do. I am not familiar with the science of the earth. Perhaps you can research the topic and on our next hike you can explain the mechanism to me."

This made him smile, standing and offering his arm to me to grasp on the descent. "Next hike? So you've enjoyed our afternoon out?" he pressed.

I shrugged. "Like I said, it is rather welcome to have friends outside of business. True friends," I added as I touched his shoulder gently.

"Perhaps one day more than friends?" he allowed.

I felt my stomach roll the same way it did when I'd eaten food that didn't agree with me. Marry this man? Allow him to truly court me? I doubted that hideous mustache would feel the same way as Cassidy's bare face and soft lips.

"As a business man, I'm sure you know better than to count your money before you make it," I chastised, taking a few steps in front of him. He laughed at this and chased after me, keeping a brisk, jovial pace the rest of the way.

Once back inside the brothel, after saying my goodbyes to Abraham, Madam Jennie found me almost instantly. She followed me into my office and shut the door behind her. "Well?" she asked as I took a seat at my desk, moving papers around.

"I told him you were on the brink of bankruptcy," I started. She became instantly still, her eyes hard and her mouth twitching at the corners.

"You did WHAT?" she basically screamed.

I raised my hand to her, silencing her. "In exchange for a piece about the profitability of the mine. He intends to buy the shares you're after, because a discovery last week revealed the mine is set to be the richest mine in the country, if not the world. He's keeping it under wraps for now, but in a month's time, he plans to collect his investors and buy the resulting shares in the west. It's going to make him one of the wealthiest men in the world, unless you beat him to it. And since you are bankrupt, how could you afford such a thing?"

Silence stretched between us, just like when Abraham learned of her alleged bankruptcy. "Louisa," she said at long last, her expression barely changed. "I hope to never be on the opposite sides of your affection. How did you manage such information from him? Never mind, I'd rather not know." Her expression changed to her normal coy, taunting one as she considered what I'd told her. At long last, she sat across from me. "Do you think there's any more information he's not sharing? How do we know these claims are valid and not him attempting to drag himself out of debt?"

I shrugged. "I suppose we don't. You have a month to make your decision, since that's when he plans on rallying his investors, if that part is true."

Madam Jennie nodded. "And you will see him again?" she pressed.

I sighed and nodded. "I supposed as much, and made a comment about wanting to see him again." I cringed as I said it.

"Oh, don't feel bad for breaking the old boy's heart, he's hardly an angel." She misread my intentions and I let her. "Well then...this is quite some information to stew on. I'll find some of my sources and see if I can locate the truth. Someone out there knows about these ores except for Abraham, I'll make it my mission to find them." With that, she left the office, closing the door gently behind her. She didn't leave her office the rest of the night.

Chapter 14

THE NEXT MORNING, I awoke to a letter from an anonymous source. No name, but an address was written in beautiful scrawl in the top left. The postage said it was from California. My heart raced as I tore open the envelope, sitting in the hallway on a bench to read its short, wonderful words:

Dearest Louisa,

I have missed you every day since I left that little township of Jerome. I know it's grown on you, just as it's grown on me. My cousins and I took the train to California and ended up just over the border when tragedy struck. Our train was held up by robbers and most of our money was taken, along with some family jewels. The police assure us they're doing everything in their power to find these men and bring them to justice. I have lost hope.

California is just as beautiful as I imagined! We're staying just a few miles from the beach in a quaint little place that you would adore. Our first gig is tonight at a bar called Gin Tin, and it's actually a tin shack! You would be surprised at the way these houses look, so different from the sticks and boards of Jerome. The ocean leaves a lovely coat of salt on everything. Perhaps you can visit one day when you pull yourself away from that place? I hope you'll join me one day soon.

    Love always,
    Cassidy

I held the letter close to my heart, equally excited for her adventure and missing her immensely. Her departure was a gaping hole in my soul that I felt every day. The brief outing with Abraham did help to lift my spirits, but nothing replaced the ache I felt for her absence. I read the letter three more times before heading down to the nearest bank and wiring her a sum of money. It would be helpful, given the robbery, an unexpected and romantic gesture.

A few hours later, Abraham came calling, something he did almost every day for the next week. He would arrive in the early afternoon, sometimes late morning, and knock on the door of the boarding house to escort me to the wash down in Mingus Valley, or an afternoon in Cottonwood or Clarkdale. The week stretched out and I returned correspondence with Cassidy, after laboring and agonizing over what to write in reply. I wanted nothing more than to beg her to let me visit, to leave this place and my lump sum of festering money and join her in California. Yet, her words about waiting to settle made sense. What help would I be as she tried to land auditions? As she found a place to live? No, I would wait until she settled—we would wait until she settled—and then I would leave this place. Perhaps in California I would finally pursue nursing school and leave this odd business behind. It wasn't meant to be permanent, after all.

A fortnight passed before Madam Jennie made her move with the mine. By that time, Abraham had been calling nearly daily, if not every other day, though not once did he try to get romantic with me. I found a great relief in that, because men did not court women for company. They did so with the prospect of marriage. Perhaps Abraham was different and the draw of having someone so like-minded to speak to was enough to keep him coming around.

Our courting didn't go without notice. The girls in the brothel often teased me about it, though all in good nature, except Tabitha. There was an almost jealous streak in the way she spoke about Abraham. "Did you hike up your skirt on your little hike?" she would titter in a way that now annoyed me to no end. At first, the idea brought a shade of red to my face, but it became such a tedious, repetitive question that I could only answer with boredom.

"You'll never truly know what being courted by a powerful man entails, it seems," I responded at last, something to silence her on the matter permanently. She still pried when she could, but found herself facing the same bland responses. Tabitha was no longer a creature I loved nor admired. I now saw her for what she was—a selfish, insolent child.

On the day Madam Jennie meant to make her purchase of the mine, I was sent down to Cottonwood to retrieve some supplies from a clothier in town. It was touted as the best place to purchase garments, for the seamstress was endlessly talented, and the quality of the fabrics came from India and beyond.

Madam Jennie placed an order some time ago and I was to retrieve it, as well as anything else I found appealing. Madam Jennie spared no expense to help clothe me, despite my protest. I was fine with the same few outfits and coats, she was not, especially now that I was so exposed to the elite with Abraham. I told Abraham we were in perpetual credit with the stores and that Jennie sold the old outfits we no longer wore. "To keep appearances," I told him sadly. He delighted in that piece of information.

The clothier was a modest looking shop in the downtown of Cottonwood, just a few steps away from the jail. "May I help you?" asked the sharply dressed woman upon my entering. Her garments were of a stunning quality and with such meticulous care even I could appreciate them. It was no wonder this place held such high popularity with the locals.

"Hello, yes, I'm here to collect some garments ordered by a Madam Jennie of Jerome."

The girl nodded, her eyes lighting up. "Ah, yes, quite a taste that one has. Come, let me grab our seamstress."

She disappeared and reappeared sometime later with Heather in tow. We both stopped in our tracks, our eyes meeting. For the briefest moment, I could see the flash of fear in her eyes, and I felt my own heart race in my chest. I hadn't seen her in months, not since she took the cash I'd stored in the house and left. That seemed like a lifetime ago, before the brothel and before Cassidy.

She was older, though still holding some of the indignant look a child generally has. She was taller and still thin as a bean, but her hair was now well managed and in a fashionable knot on her head. "Heather," I managed at last.

"Louisa," she responded, her voice choked in her throat. The woman looked between us awkwardly before dismissing herself with a mutter, leaving us relatively alone in the back of the store.

"So you went to work for Madam Jennie," she said, more a statement than a question.

"I did, yes, as a bookkeeper," I responded. She nodded, though something about her look made me wonder if she believed me. "And you're here, as a seamstress?"

She nodded again, chewing her bottom lip. "It was a great opportunity," she allowed.

"Yes, I imagine so," I replied, and silence lapsed between us.

"I have Madam Jennie's garments here, if you'd like to see them. I...I might have something you'd like as well." She said it shyly, placing the garments on the table next to her before disappearing into another back room. I was worried that she wouldn't return, and relief flooded me when she popped back around the corner a few minutes later. She motioned for me to step into another room and closed the door, handing me a blue fabric so exquisite I couldn't stop my fingers as they reached out to touch it.

"The blue would look great with your hair, I think. I thought of you when I saw it, but I wasn't sure how you felt about my leaving with all the money."

I laughed a short bark of a laugh, turning the fabric over in my hand. "It was hardly any amount of the money, truly. I have it stored in so many places for safety, I'm sorry for being dishonest with that. It turned out to be an appropriate decision though."

She gave her own small laugh, shrugging at the thought. "I should have expected as much from you. Always so cautious."

Silence passed again, then she motioned for me to try on the garment. It was a coat and skirt combination, and I was surprised at how light the fabric felt despite its intricate design and coloration. I expected it to be heavy and drab like most fabric but it hung loose and cool, promising free movement. I was surprised, too, to see that it fitted me modestly. Some of the garment makers did not understand the lay of my body and often made me look obscene with the dips of the waist and constraints of the fabric. This was flattering and brought out the color of my eyes.

"Please, take it... An olive branch?" she said at last, content that I was satisfied by the fabric.

"Are you positive?" I asked, reluctant to part with the fabric.

She nodded. "Louisa, I...I do miss you. But I hope you can know that I am happy here. This is what I enjoy doing," she said with great hesitation, as though I might disapprove.

"I shall visit when I can, I think. We have much to catch up on." I almost told her then about Cassidy, about Abraham, about the mine, but I kept it to myself. I finished up with my purchases with a promise to call on her in the coming week and took a carriage back to Jerome.

Abraham was waiting for me outside the brothel, pacing back and forth in short strides. His eyes were dark and those thick, caterpillar eyebrows were pulled so tightly together they finally met in the middle of his forehead. It didn't take me long to realize why, so I took my time unloading the items from the carriage and instructing the various staff to carry different items to different rooms or places. Abraham stood precariously close during this entire event, his mood palpable in the air.

At last, the items returned and the carriage driver paid, I turned to look to Abraham. "Hello Abraham," I greeted. He frowned.

"Do not 'hello Abraham' me as though you don't know very well why I'm here!" His voice rose in the middle of the street, which was busy with the supper crowd, drawing stares. I was content to let him have his say in the street, let him scream at a woman in public, but he had enough sense to lower his voice to just a contained simmer. "If there's somewhere more private we can converse," he said, the veins in his neck standing out.

"Of course, follow me," I said, heading into the brothel and to my office. On the way through the foyer, I passed Celeste, who watched with barely concealed curiosity, and followed us down the hallway and took a seat on the bench outside my office. I gave her a thankful look as I closed the door to my office, pointing to the chair for him to sit. He didn't, but at least waited for me to be seated behind my desk before launching into his tirade.

"Was that your plan the entire time, hmm? To distract me from making my purchase of the mine so Madam Jennie could...could SWOOP in and buy my rightful shares?" His voice rose to such a clamor I doubted the walls of the office did much to keep the house out of our conversation. "And all this time I thought we were something more. I was courting you for the love of God! You should be thankful for the attention, honestly, it's not exactly as though you're a handsome woman! I saw a grand opportunity for us to be business partners, perhaps partners in life, and I told you what I did about the mine in confidence!" He was visibly shaking, pacing the small office, his rage rolling off him in great waves.

In the face of his anger, I felt an odd sense of calm settle over me. It was different than when others would get mad, behind closed doors and thin smiles. This outright display of anger was soothing to me. I didn't need to get a word in, he spoke for both of us. His shoulders rolled and he continued to pace, spewing hateful remark after hateful remark.

At long last, after what felt like an eternity, he quieted down and stared at me full on. "Have you nothing to say for yourself?" he asked, shocked.

"I think you've said enough for both of us," I said. This started his rage again once more.

"I've never been spoken to so disrespectfully in my life!" he hissed.

My head jerked up to glare at him. "You wouldn't survive a day as a woman, then. I'd show you the door but I believe you know where it is."

He stopped and stared in stunned silence, his jaw slack, his eyes wide. "You will regret this to your dying day," he said at last, a phrase he nearly spat at me, before turning to storm out of the office, not bothering to close the door.

A full twenty seconds of silence passed before Madam Jennie appeared in the same doorway, a smirk on her face. "A warning would have been nice," I said, feeling the anger start to build up, delayed but potent.

"I did warn you," she said, closing the door behind her and sitting in the seat Abraham refused.

"Yes, weeks ago. I hadn't heard a thing since," I retorted.

She shrugged in her noncommittal way. "What's done is done. I take it he's very angry?" she asked, a smile sliding over her face.

I couldn't help but smile as well. "The purchase went through?" I asked.

"Oh yes, better than expected. It seems my sources agreed with what he'd told you. A copious vein was found just a few weeks ago and the miners who found it were paid very heavily to keep it a secret. Nothing like some alcohol and a beautiful woman to peel such a secret from a man, though. The man selling his shares was unaware of the discovery and let all his shares go for a smaller price than he intended. I did throw in some...extra perks."

"And Abraham?" I asked.

She shrugged again. "He'll come out all right. There's no great blow to him, if anything, he has an extra backer. He'll soon calm down once he realizes what a great deal has been struck. Sure, he's not as rich as he would like, but us? You and I are on our way up and out." She leaned back in the chair, steepling her fingers.

"Up and out," I agreed, unsure where 'out' was for me.

Dearest Cassidy,

Things have been quite entertaining in Jerome and at the brothel. The renovation of the second brothel is complete, and we're now having two separate houses boast entertainment. We've also expanded the foyer to include a real stage, so when you return, you'll be like a true star. I do hope you return and play one last time before you become famous.

The mine is exploding, figuratively of course. A vein was found and the information of its spoils will be released about the same time you receive my letter. This vein is said to carry the mine for the next few decades and will be the richest in the world. The thought is so perplexing to me. When we traveled here from Kansas, Jerome was just an afterthought. It's a shore we washed up on, and now it's on the precipice of greatness. Madam Jennie predicts it will draw even more men and women to Jerome and we'll soon be a bustling city.

I also ran into Heather in Cottonwood the other day. She's a true seamstress it seems, working with fabrics so exquisite I cannot even put them into words. Instead, I sent you one, which I hope you find to your liking. I did my best to guess your measurements, but a talented seamstress can fashion it into something more fitting if you require.

Winter is coming, the chill can be felt in the air at night. Next week is the annual Hallows Eve Ball, held at Spooky Hall, which I've never attended before. It should be entertaining, given we purchased the mine out from under Abraham. I hope his odd personality has him on the out with the rest of the elite and I won't be such an outlier at the party. I fear, though, I am always an outlier without you.

With love,
Your Louisa

Chapter 15

THE OCTOBER BALL came on a bright, cool day, the first of the coming autumn. Fall in Jerome snuck up very slowly, and then when it hit, it did so with full force. The temperature would drop to a chill overnight, as though someone opened the door to autumn. Winter wouldn't be too far behind, though it was mild enough to be seen as a continuation of autumn. At long last, spring would come in a hurried rush, sprinting toward the stifling summers.

The day of the October ball was just this way, the first day of cool temperatures. It drove most men and women to layer their coats and blouses to levels seen in snowing populations. I remembered the winter clothes we'd brought from Kansas and how useless they became in here. Heather turned them into an assortment of clothes more suited for the temperate climate. Now, neither of us would want for appropriate clothes; we both had the means to secure it. She sent me a dress just for the occasion, something that could be partially removed in the heat of a ball and re-applied in the cool of the night.

Heather, it seemed, had moved from seamstress to inventor

of styles. Just earlier that week, she'd mentioned adding a hood to some outfits—a dated idea, truly—but for the purpose of shielding you from the rain. She assured me the final project would be something marvelous and new, but I didn't hold my breath.

Madam Jennie and I gathered our things about us and set out for the ball, which was only a few blocks away and easier to travel by foot than carriage. The carriages were lined up the Main Street nearly to our boarding house anyway, and Madam Jennie preferred to travel with me than from her house on the hill. She'd spent much time up there as of late, doing God knows what, but the brothel didn't suffer in her absence. It had me to run it, everything from the silly squabbles between the girls to any issues that arose with the staff.

Spooky's Hall was decorated to the nines for the October ball. While it didn't claim to commemorate any holiday in particular, it was obvious that the homage was to Halloween. The decorations mirrored what autumn would look like if Jerome ever bothered to get cold enough. The trees were changing, true, but in other places, they were long since dead and wilted. There was a hopeful sense of life in our autumn, where others associated it with death. Even my garden held out against the onslaught of temperature changes. My summer plants still grew strong and my winter ones were coming in with the same fervor. I spent many an afternoon alone in the garden, sitting amongst its lush piles, trying to decide how best to attack a winter that may or may not come.

Our arrival was announced at the entrance of the door and a hush fell over the crowd, which was large enough in size for such a silence to be noticeable. The ball had officially started just an hour prior and only appeared to be at half capacity. I scanned the crowd quickly for Abraham and did not see him.

Perhaps he wasn't here yet, or perhaps he wouldn't come at all. Something about his parting words to me still hung in the air, but I doubted his ability to make a meaningful move against me. What could he do, truly? Nothing that would harm me and still leave his reputation intact.

The ball was boring. Madam Jennie floated amongst a crowd that congratulated her success with one breath and criticized her with another behind her back. When I separated from her to wander the halls and play a game of cards here and there I could hear it—a woman who owned whores now owned a chunk of the mine. Some gossiped over the news about the mine and its profitability. I ignored most of it, and after merely an hour and a half at the ball, I excused myself for home. Madam Jennie did not seem particularly surprised or upset to see me go, she was having a lavish time fighting off suitors of men. Those who had previously abandoned the idea of marrying her were back in full force with the knowledge of her success and finances. She was a hot commodity once more, and I was glad for the anonymity to escape unseen.

The sun set ungodly early during these nights. Overhead, the street lights cast a subtle glow that did more to add shadows than to dispel the dark. I wondered idly over many topics; when I would see Heather next, when I would leave Jerome for California, how Cassidy was doing. I almost didn't notice the shifting of the shadows to my side, but the movement was enough to cause me to start and snap my head to the side. There, through the gaps in the businesses, a shadow of a man was undoubtedly following me.

"Abraham," I called, feeling rather annoyed by the situation. He was notably absent from the ball and now he was following me through the streets? The man was as frustrating as he was ugly. Who emerged from the shadows, however, was not Abraham. It was a man I did not recognize. He was taller than Abraham and wider than a Clydesdale, looking all meat and no nicety. My heart raced in my chest, wishing I wasn't wearing such fashionable clothing. It was so restrictive to be so well dressed. I longed instantly for my thinner silks from my poor days.

"Not Abraham," he said, a slow smile spreading across his face. "You are Louisa, no one could miss that ugly face."

I took a step back, looking around frantically. The ball drew the crowd to the street a block or two away, this part of the street was deserted. I was alone. "What do you want?" I asked, fighting to keep my voice level.

"He said you'd regret it," he pressed. His hand moved and I saw him reaching for his gun on his hip with the holster and I let out a scream. No one came. He laughed, pulling the gun out and aiming it at me. "Run," he suggested, cocking the gun loudly.

I did what was requested. I turned and ran in the direction of the brothel. The first shot rang out horribly close to my head and I covered it, still running in the general direction of the brothel. The next one whizzed past my arm, cutting through the fabric of my clothing and tearing it. He laughed as I cried out and almost fell to the ground. The next shot actually made purchase with the meat of my arm, bringing me to my knees.

My heart was racing in my ears and tears stained my face at both the pain and horror of the situation. Is this really how I was to die? Gunned down in the street like some animal? I stumbled to my feet again and made a few lurching attempts, hearing another gunshot sing out and miss me. A grunt from behind me caused me to hesitate and turn, watching two figures mercilessly attack the man with the gun. In the shadows cast by the light, they were undeniably women, and undeniably of the brothel type given their dress. I realized how close we were to the brothel then and thanked every star in the sky.

I stumbled in the direction of the group in time to see that Tabitha was one of the girls, holding a bit of wood in her hands like a sword. She'd slammed it into some part of his body to bring him to his knees, and then again on the back of his head. He fell forward into the dirt with a loud thump. By this time, the gunshots brought a few people in the neighboring streets out to investigate, though they kept their distance. "Ring the police!" screamed the second girl, who I recognized as Celeste. She also held a plank in her hand, though she dropped it to the ground then. No one in the crowd moved, so she yelled louder, "Go ring the police! This man shot this woman!"

Tabitha joined in then, tossing her board aside with more emphasis than Celeste. "Ya heard her, are ya daft? Grab the police!" A few people scuttled away, hopefully to get the authorities, though I didn't count on it.

I stumbled toward them and Celeste grabbed my arm to steady me. "Are you okay, Louisa? What's going on?" I shook my head, my hand still over my bleeding arm. "Are you bleeding? Did he shoot you?!" She was pulling me then, dragging me to the new doctor's office down the street. I'd never been. Most maladies I could manage on my own with my herbs and my Ma's book, but Celeste wasn't taking any refusal from me. She banged on the door of the office until it opened up.

I don't remember much else of the night, as I was so incapacitated with pain. I wavered in and out of consciousness as the bullet was pulled from my arm and my arm was bandaged and set. I heard various discussion about infection, broken arm, casting...none of it made any sense.

All I knew is that when I awoke the next morning in my own bed, my arm hurt something fierce, but I was alive.

My life became a never ending plague of worry. The man was apprehended but confessed to nothing. He was jailed for attempted murder but disappeared the first night in jail, as did the rest of the men jailed with him. Rumor was that it was an inside job, but no one really cared. After all, my association to the brothel likened me with sin and all the other unmentionable acts that occurred there. No real emphasis was placed on finding him or the other escaped men in the jail that night.

I spent a few days in bed before the act of doing nothing turned me sour and unmanageable. Thankfully, my left arm was taken out and I was right handed, so I was able to return to work to take my mind off the endless dull throb in my arm. I made a poultice for pain and healing and to prevent infection using my own resources after seeing the chop job the doctor had done. The stitches were too tight and the entire thing looked massacred. I didn't want to imagine how hideous the scar would be.

My garden went a week unattended but I was too terrified to go visit it. When I finally worked up the nerve, I dressed in an outfit that concealed my looks entirely, took a carriage half way, took back roads and streets the rest of the way, crisscrossing so I couldn't be followed. At long last, I was in the garden and sobbed into the beautiful plants that shielded me from the prying eyes of the neighbors and the street.

I don't know why Tabitha and Celeste did what they did. They both claimed they were outside having a smoke when they heard the gunshots. They didn't know it was me, just that a woman was running away from a man holding a gun. They found some boards on the side of the street from previous construction and took him out while he was unaware. They tried to tend to me as best as they could, even Tabitha suspending her usual taunting of me to be kind and bring me food. Celeste, Veronica, and a few of the other women tried their best to make me comfortable while I sat in abject misery in my bed. It was kind of them, I suppose a way to return the favor of all the various concoctions I made up for them over the last few months. Cold remedies, cuts and scrapes, everything really. I even helped one of the younger girls with her acne. It still surprised me to see the outflow of support they gave me since I wasn't particularly close to any of them.

The man was at large, no one would believe my account about Abraham, and I was left at a loss about what to do. I sat in the garden and drew lines in the dirt for a few hours before an idea—a strange, small idea—began to form. I smiled to myself and dug up any and all the pots of money I had hidden in the garden and began to catalogue my finances.

Chapter 16

TWO DAYS LATER, after I'd decided to enact my plan, I found an envelope on my desk. There were no words on it save my name, no stamp, no evidence that it had come with the mail. I flagged down one of the staff members, who claimed a man left it on the porch with instructions to deliver it to me. I returned to my desk and closed the door to my office, opening it slowly.

Inside was just a newspaper clipping from the San Diego Harold. It was dated a week prior, and the headline read "Local Married Couple Hits Big With Opening." Under the title was a picture of Cassidy and her cousin, though they were standing too close together, and he was kissing her on the cheek. Above them was a banner at a venue with the words "The Jones Band" in block letters.

Mrs. Cassidy Jones and her husband, John Jones, from San Diego California hit it big with their opening number just a week before. The couple just returned from a country wide tour and drummed up support with their unique style of saloon music that captivated America as a whole. Upon their return to California, they were welcomed to the Congress Hotel, long known for hosting big name acts in music. They begin a three week stay here with promise for many more shows as they play to sold out shows every night.

"It's a blessing," says Mrs. Jones, who's been married to John for three years now. The San Diego native is known for her short hair and high pitched voice. Mr. Jones, from San Francisco, says the change in pace from up north to the south is welcome. "The ocean is beautiful down here, and it's great for her voice. I've heard her sing all across the nation and this is our big chance."

Watch the happy couple perform Thursday through Sunday at the Old Congress Hotel at 9pm.

I put the article down, not really understanding what it said at first. Married? No, it must be a mistake. I looked at the picture of them again and wondered how I could have missed it when they were in town. They looked nothing alike. The way she placed a hand on his chest, the way he leaned into her...and from California? There was no way this was true. She was from Boston! Her accent! The stories she told about the city!

I got up and paced my office, worrying over the article... but, furthermore, wondering who the hell sent it to me. Who would know of my relationship with Cassidy? It was not as though we left together. Was it one of the women in the brothel? I considered this, but who was cruel enough? Tabitha? No, she wouldn't have come to my aide if she had such ill will toward me... A man dropped it off. Could it have been Abraham?

I felt the edges of my nerves fray even more and temporarily hamper any plans I had set into motion. I needed to see for myself. I needed to ask her to her face what was going on. If he was her husband so be it, but what did that mean for us? Why would she invite me to California? Why would she...

I looked down at the tally I'd been making about my finances in attempt to set them straight. With the money hidden all over Jerome and Cottonwood, it'd taken a lot of work to sort out exactly how much I had. Enough, plenty really, but some of the tallies were in categories of their own. Money sent to Cassidy. Hundreds of dollars. Fine clothing, gifts... In the two and a half months she'd been gone, she received more than what Pa made in a year. Did she play me for my money? No, she never asked for any... She didn't have to.

Anger, hurt, betrayal...it flashed over me like a cold bath. I knew then what I had to do. I tallied some money off into a separate category and, once level headed, went about making my plans for the now. It was just a temporary delay to my plans but I needed to do this first.

"Kansas?" Madam Jennie asked, looking over the edge of her glasses at me. She rarely wore them, except when she was up all night going over paperwork. She'd been doing that a lot more lately with the purchase of nearly half the mine. It involved a lot of moving things around, I supposed, before they finalized what they needed. The idea was to start the first phase of the plan to mine the new vein at the turn of the year, hoping to have the first batch of its success by mid-February.

"Yes, Kansas. To see family for the holidays. My aunt has become ill," I said. I handed her a letter describing the details of my invented aunt's illness with pleas to see her for the last time. It also inquired after my Pa, a touch I hoped wasn't too heavy handed. Jennie knew the extent of my orphan status more so than anyone else did, she'd realize how important it would be for me to return to Kansas to see an aunt who still thought her brother was still alive. "Just a little over a week, perhaps two at the most. It will depend on the weather and the trains, as you know, travel is hardly predictable."

She nodded, "Very well," she said, dismissing me.

Within two days, I had two tickets in my hand, one for San Diego and one for Kansas. I handed the man at the podium my ticket to Kansas and walked three carts down, exiting the train at the edge of the platform. I waited for the train to pull away before going to another platform to board the train to San Diego. My identification was forged but there was no one to recognize me or care. In between trains, I applied a thick powder to my hair and eyebrows that turned it from its normal blood red to a dark brown. It would wash out easy enough, but it was just the disguise needed. A brunette with sparse freckles and modest clothing would be ignored and overlooked. Louisa, the red head, would stick out.

This train was one of the newer high speed trains which topped speeds of 80 mph. The train would reach San Diego in a few hours, giving me enough time to study the map and the information I had gathered. Notes I'd taken of Cassidy's letters sat in my lap, pressed flat to study them for any clues to connect to the article in the newspaper. Nothing jumped out. I did have some details I could investigate—her favorite breakfast place, her favorite clothier. She rather enjoyed a certain spot on the beach. I wondered if any of these were lies, but a bigger part of me wanted it all to be a big misunderstanding. Perhaps the paper mistook them for a couple? Or their origin? Or else they mixed up the photograph? There had to be a mistake some-where, if I only looked hard enough.

I also had the newspaper clipping. Well, parts of it. In a rage, I tore it into pieces and sobbed with abandon in my garden. After a moment to collect, I reassembled the pieces as best as I could, pasting them together with haphazard care. At last, it resembled the paper before, but the words remained unchanged—married. Local. I would settle this once and for all.

I arrived in San Diego shortly after 5pm and checked into my inn for the night. It was then I realized that Jerome had no inns, just boarding houses, likely due to the lack of tourism. Anyone who came to Jerome did so to live, hence the grand assortment of boarding houses and entertainment for the locals. There was nothing to lure tourists to the air that perpet-ually smelled of smelter or the line of saloons and brothels.

In the morning, I awoke early, fashioned my hair mostly hidden in a hat, and reapplied the powder in a way to hide the bits that stuck out as brown instead of red. My arm wasn't fully healed yet and still in a sling but I could hide that under my jacket. The hair was a good disguise, but with a visible ailment, I would be easier to notice.

I set out to the beach that morning and was shocked at how large it was. No wonder my mother wished to see it before she died. I stood and marveled at the great expanse of it, up and down an entire coast! It took a full fifteen minutes before I could pull myself from my shock and journey down the street to the breakfast nook Cassidy wrote about in her letters. I sat at a table outside so I could easily see those who came and went and ordered, reading a book to pass the time.

Within thirty minutes time, I saw her.

She still had that sassy short hair and that swing to her hips that I adored so much. I began to stand with every intention to approach her until I realized she wasn't alone. John, her husband-cousin, was holding her hand and laughing as they got a seat a few tables away from me. I was out of their line of sight but they were very much in mine. I watched them interact and laugh, touch each other's hands, caress each other's arms. Open displays of affection, no hint of her Boston accent. And on her left ring finger sat a simple band, one that I remembered being around her neck on a necklace. "From my mama before she died," she told me sadly. Now it sat on her finger as a proud declaration of her marriage.

After a short time, John left, tipping his hat to her, and Cassidy left shortly after. I paid my own bill and followed her at a safe distance up the streets to her house. I *knew* she lived in a small cottage near the sea with her *cousins* but I didn't know where. If she came on foot, it couldn't have been too far. I kept a steady pace behind her, glad for my choice of sensible shoes without a heel to keep my presence unknown.

Within four blocks, she disappeared into a small cottage. The beach was four blocks down the way, another lie, but this cottage still had its appeal. Small, quiet, but beautiful and well maintained with exotic plants in the front. I stood across the street, thinking hard over what I was going to say. I rehearsed it over and over the night before and the walk here. I would demand her to tell me the truth, be honest with me. I needed to hear it from her lips before I could leave.

After what seemed like an eternity, I gathered my will and strode across the street, knocking on the door with enough force to ensure she'd answer it. "Yes?" she asked, peeking around the door. She studied my face for a few seconds before her eyes widened. "Louisa...is that you?" Was that fear in her eyes? Or surprise? Or love? I tried to keep my eyes voice as I smiled.

"Surprise!" I greeted. She stood there a full thirty seconds and we just stared at each other. "Well, are you going to let me in? Show me around?" I pressed. She moved to the side and I walked in, looking around.

The proof of her lies were everywhere.

Pictures, portraits, framed proclamations of her marriage to John were all over the walls. The cottage was decorated in the fashion of a place that was well lived in, and had been for quite some time, more than a few months. Her lies were dripping off the walls and made my right fist clench under my coat. "What a surprise," she said, painfully aware of my roving eyes. "What brings you out here?" she asked.

"The truth," I said at long last, turning to her. I pulled the article from where it was stored in my satchel and handed it to her. She took it gingerly in her hands, running a finger over the ripped pieces.

"I see," she said. "Come to the kitchen, we can talk in there." She set the paper down on a table as she headed to the kitchen and motioned for me to take a seat. I did so slowly, unable to fully relax. She went to the cupboard to grab cups. "Can I get you some water? Lemonade?"

"No," I replied, a little more curt than I intended. She

sighed and took a seat across from me.

"What do you want to know?" she asked.

I laughed. "Everything. What's the truth? What are the lies? Why..." I felt my voice crack and I swallowed. "How you could do this to me," I finished, feeling my face heat in shame and anger. Cassidy looked down at her hands and sighed.

"Louisa, I'm surprised you didn't figure it out before. You're a smart girl, you have a lot of business savvy...but it didn't take long to see your weakness. No one loved you, not truly. No one paid an ounce of attention to you. The minute someone did, like Tabitha, you ate it up. All I had to do was pretend," I visibly flinched at that word, "to care about you and you were mine. You were telling me secrets of Jerome that no outsider could ever hope to know! And your money," she laughed. "Oh your money! I knew the minute we got to that brothel that you were the brains behind it! And seeing how well that place was done up, the reputation Madam Jennie had for her riches. Originally, our plan was for me to ask to stay at her place on the hill and rob her blind. After I met you, after we spoke, I knew you'd freely give me money if I asked, and no crime would follow us. It didn't take more than a second to make up a backstory and you were hooked."

I could feel that odd, ancient sensation of tears welling up in the back of my eyes and I did everything to force them back. I would not cry for her again, especially not in front of her. I wished I'd never ripped that paper up, never shown my weakness to her. "So you're not from Boston?" I asked when I found my voice.

She laughed and leaned back in her chair. "Heavens, no! San Diego, and John is from San Francisco. We were traveling the country and had just come from the deep south. It seemed an easy enough cover to make it to the cities we went to. Those we robbed, oh definitely, but stealing money gets old and boring. There's tracks to cover and care to be taken. With you? It was easy money, and just what we needed to return home." She shrugged then, standing to go to the sink.

"I'm not sure what you thought, Louisa. That I could care for someone like you? Love you? Even if that were...how I was, you know...I wouldn't have picked you. You are always the victim, it gets tiresome. I couldn't stay any longer and watch you pout and simper over the injustice of the world." She scoffed then, turning her back to me to rummage through a drawer.

Something cracked in my chest. Ma was dead, she'd died on the way to this horrific state. Pa died shortly after in a fire, and we'd never recover his body. Heather left me. Abraham tried to have me killed and the police didn't care, Madam Jennie didn't even care. Cassidy, the one person I thought loved and cared for me, was a fraud. A con artist. A thief. She didn't stop at trying to rob me, she decided to destroy my heart in the process.

And she was still speaking.

"Now that Tabitha girl, she would have been more my style if I were going to gamble my life for the love of a woman. You were an easy necessity; it wasn't hard to do. A few kisses, some proclamations of love, really, it was like dating a school aged boy. And you didn't know any better!" She shook her head, her back still to me. I didn't recognize her voice without the accent, it felt like someone else was telling me this story. Someone who was not Cassidy.

I don't know how it happened, but one minute she was talking and the next minute she was silent.

I wasn't sitting anymore. I was standing in front of her. Her blue eyes were wide with shock as she looked up at me.

How did she get so close? When did I move across the kitchen? I felt something warm on my hand and looked down to see dark red sticky liquid all over my right hand. It clasped the handle of a knife that was buried to the hilt in her abdomen.

How did it get there? She looked at me, shock and pain on her face, her mouth open in a silent "oh." Her blood continued to run from the wound and over my hands, down her dress, onto the floor. It was a steady stream, too steady to support life. I took a step back as her knees buckled and she fell to the floor on them. I'm sure this is what I looked like when I'd been shot, grasping at the wound helplessly, trying to fill the void left by a weapon. Trying to stop the steady pour of blood. Trying and failing. She looked pathetic.

Cassidy looked up at me, those beautiful eyes wide, but I did nothing to help her. "Louisa," she whispered. Her voice was thick with pain and her chest rose and fell rapidly as she gasped for air. "Louisa...help..." she reached out for me and I took a step back. The blood sickened me, as did her face and everything about her in that moment. Where I once saw beauty, now I only saw deceit, lies, filth. Her out of fashion short hair made her look like she was trying too hard. Her dress was plain, proof she wasn't talented enough to buy expensive clothes. Her home, this home! Not even on the beach.

I watched her struggle some more, her hand weak on the hilt of the knife. I watched the blood begin to slow. I saw her face turn a ghastly shade of white as she crumpled to the side. She continued to stare up at me with her mouth gaping like a fish as she tried to form words. Eventually, her chest stopped rising and falling. The puddle that surrounded her was too wide for her to still be alive but I was too disgusted by her bleeding body to check for life.

Instead, I went around the cottage. I smashed every picture

I could find. I tore their wedding shroud, I ripped books apart. I went through every room and destroyed anything and everything I could find. I hesitated only at her jewelry chest, where I took every bit of jewelry from the collection. It was quite a bit, some pieces too expensive for her to afford on her own. More of her lies, more of her deceit, things she stole from others who didn't know her true nature.

I went through their things and took money, took valuables, stashed them all in my purse. I ruined and destroyed what I could. And, as a final touch, I broke the lock on the back door.

I may have been made temporarily feral, but I wasn't stupid.

Lastly, I started up a fire in the fireplace and burnt the newspaper clipping that was sent to me and watched it burst into flames. I left the fire burning, hoping it would burn her with it, hoping it would turn her into ash and take down the entire neighborhood with it. I hoped they all suffered for knowing her, just the way I did.

At long last, I slipped out the back door just as the sun was reaching mid-afternoon, leaving it wide open, and started in the direction of my inn.

On the way, it occurred to me that I was hungry, so I stopped at a diner and ate there alone. The food was the most delicious food I had tasted in what felt like years. After I'd eaten my fill, I went to my inn, bathed, and slept long and hard for the first time in weeks.

Chapter 17

I'D TOLD Madam Jennie I would be gone a week or more, but I'd accomplished what I wanted to the first day in San Diego. No, I did not anticipate...that...happening. And honestly, I wasn't sure what *that* was. The next day, in the paper there was nothing about a quaint cottage on the ocean shore with a grisly murder that occurred. Maybe, I'd imagined it all. Maybe, I hadn't even left bed. I remembered being there as though I were in a fog. If it weren't for the blood I scrubbed from under my fingernails or the stains on my dress, I would have thought it a dream.

Still, I had a week or more to spend my time, so I spent it well. That morning, I put on my disguise and went to the beach. It was a cold day, cold enough to require an overcoat, and slightly overcast. The warmth of Arizona was long gone and replaced with a bitter chill from the ocean breeze. I sat in the sand, watching the waves roll in and out. There weren't too many people around me due to the weather, and those that were out stayed far from the water like I was.

How strange was it that I was looking at the very ocean Ma

wished to see? It was her one real reason for coming to California over any of the other places those with consumption went. She wanted to see the ocean, and now I was seeing it for her. I felt tears well up in the back of my eyes and for once, I let them fall, silent and slow, down my face. I sat like that for many hours until curiosity overtook me and I ventured to the water.

The cold was an utter shock that cut me to the core. It traveled up my feet and curled around my heart, causing my breath to catch in my lungs. But it was so delightful paired with the wind, I took off my hat and let my long, red hair fly free. I didn't care about being noticed then. Who was going to know? Who was going to see a red haired girl in a sea of strange people and know it was me, Louisa, from tiny Jerome, Arizona. Not Louisa from Kansas either, she was long gone.

I spent the afternoon sorting through the things I stole from Cassidy's home, deciding what to keep and what to sell. It was easy enough, some of the pieces were so exquisite they couldn't be sold without considerable attention. Others were commonplace and could easily be pawned. Perhaps I'd keep some as a family heirloom. The idea of my having a family made me laugh.

The next morning, I lay in bed until well into the afternoon, then roused myself for breakfast at Cassidy's favorite place. It's there I spotted the headline of the papers, "Local Woman Grisly Murder." I bought a paper for myself and read through the article over breakfast.

Mrs. Cassidy Jones of San Diego, California was found murdered in a grisly way on the night of Monday the 23rd. Her husband, a John Jones, came home to find their house broken into through the back door and robbed thoroughly. A fire was burning in the fireplace meant to burn the whole building down. He found his wife murdered by knife in the kitchen in a most ghastly manner.

Police have no leads currently but have interviewed countless neighbors to find what man could be responsible for this. "I can't believe this happened in our neighborhood!" said a Miss Ronda Howe, a neighbor of the Joneses. She said she knew the couple well and liked them immensely.

The Joneses reached local fame recently for their singing career, including a few week gig at the Old Congress Hotel. They were set to perform on Thursday.

Mr. Jones was not available for comment.

Police have warned to be on the lookout for a man described at 5'8 with a mustache who was seen in the neighborhood about the time of the break in.

A man. A man! I could have laughed at the absurdity of it all. I felt relief, I realized, relief that I would not be caught. "It's a shame, isn't it?" asked the waitress as she set my food down before me.

"Excuse me?" I asked, looking up at her. She waved her hand to the paper.

"Things like that don't happen in towns like this. San Diego is a safe place." She shook her head and walked away.

Luckily for them, I had a train ticket to take me to San

Francisco that afternoon, ensuring San Diego was once again a safe place.

It had been almost a week and a half before I was in Jerome again. My train pulled into the station a little after 4pm and I exited without anyone to meet me. I coordinated a train that arrived around relatively the same time as one from Kansas, just in case anyone was monitoring my movements that closely. I doubted it, but after the unsuccessful attempt on my life, I wasn't about to drop my guard.

Returning to the boarding house and brothel was a strange feeling. I simultaneously felt like I'd been gone years and like I'd never left at all. Everything passed in slow motion, rose colored glass, disjointed movements. I didn't see much of anyone as I climbed the stairs to my room and unlocked the door.

The minute I entered my room, I knew something was amiss. Something about the room was changed, as though it'd been passed through multiple times. Small changes I noticed— a sheet shifted just a bit to the left, a pillow with the ends facing the wrong way. Someone went through great pains to make sure it looked as though my room was untouched.

Thankfully, I'd cleared much of my valuables from the room before I left. My ledger with an entire analysis and log of my finances stayed with me at all times. My plans were mostly contrived in my head, my research wasn't anywhere that could be readily found. I hoped whoever looked through my things found nothing and felt ridiculous for it.

I did instinctively reach for Ma's nursing book and rifle through it. It was untouched, in the sense that nothing was missing, but that didn't mean it hadn't been copied. So what if someone found out the ingredients to the potions? I had a higher calling in the brothel than that, didn't I? Also, it was missing some key features that made it bearable to taste and more efficient at working, so if anyone tried to mimic the recipe, they'd be in for a sour surprise. That alone made me happy.

"You're home," said Madam Jennie from the doorway, making me jump.

I replaced the book on the shelf and turned to look at her, smiling. "Yes, it's good to be back," I replied.

She nodded, watching me carefully. "I trust your trip was well?" she pressed.

I nodded, beginning to take off my traveling attire. "It was, at least the travel was. My family was just as it always is, unbearable." I shrugged then, taking off my jacket and placing it to the side to wash later.

"Did you see Heather?" she asked. This gave me pause.

"No," I replied, honest for once. She sent me to collect the clothing from that shop in Clarksdale, she must have known she would be there. "She actually never left Arizona territory. She's working at that fine shop in Clarkdale, the one with the impressive linens. I'm surprised you haven't seen her in all your dealings. I assumed that's why you sent me to collect items," I said carefully.

She nodded slowly, tapping her jaw. "I suppose I have. Must have forgotten how she looked."

A long silence stretched between us.

"It's great to have you back. We have a lot of work to do before mining the vein after the turn of the year," she said.

"Ah, yes, I've been thinking over that," I said.

"Have you?" she pressed, interested.

"Yes, with the new vein, it's going to take more resources. More men. More interest. It might behoove us to build some boarding houses to accommodate them. Then there's consideration to the extra resources the mine itself will pull...railway, water, other resources..." I trailed off and offered a shrug. "Perhaps we should sit down with Mr. Abraham and discuss these things."

"Should we?" she asked, her gaze turning to my arm, which still hung awkwardly at my side.

"Perhaps if we make him an offer he can't refuse he will stop his silly pursuit on my life," I suggested.

Madam Jennie nodded at that. "I've much to think on," she said, turning to descend the stairs.

Yes, as did I.

Two days later, Madam Jennie peeked into my office, a strange look on her face. "I've taken what you've said into consideration, and I think you're right. We need to meet with Mr. Abraham." I nodded, feeling my heart speed up in my chest. Somehow, I'd learned to reign in the sensation of blood rushing to my face.

"I was hoping you'd agree, so I've been doing some research of my own about other purchases to consider." Madam Jennie raised a single eyebrow that reminded me so much of Cassidy I felt my breath catch in my throat. I swallowed and pressed on, "Mostly because our current situation cannot support the growth of the mine. Water rights, railroad, smelter...the whole lot of it cannot support any substantial growth."

She nodded. "I see, and I agree. Let's plan to meet with him middle of next week."

Chapter 18

THE DAY of the meeting came and I was well prepared with my documents, some of which I'd altered. Miss Jennie and I loaded up into a carriage and made our way up the hill to her house, which I'd previously never been to. She was silent the entire drive but did eye my immense pile of papers curiously.

The inside of her house was just as extravagant as the outside—three stories perched on the edge of the hill, overlooking both Jerome and the Verde Valley as it spread along the horizon. Inside, the furniture was nicer than anything in the brothel, with tall ceilings and beautiful paintings on the wall. Madam Jennie lead the way to an office and allowed me some time to organize my papers while she went about ordering the kitchen staff to make some food for us during the meeting. She poured some wine, which I declined, and settled back to wait.

Abraham arrived exactly two minutes past the hour, a sour look on his face. It was clear where he stood on the little alliance between Jennie and himself, and the way he looked at me wasn't easy to hide. Pure loathing, radiating off his thick mustache with such intensity I could feel it in my soul.

"Mister Abraham," I greeted, which he ignored. I wondered if he brought a pistol to finish the job of killing me himself. Instead, he paced to the opposite side of the table and sat down unhappily.

"Yes, hello Mr. Abraham. May I offer you a drink?" asked Madam Jennie, her tone clearly amused.

"No, let's get on with this...business meeting." He said the last bit in a resigned tone. Madam Jennie simply nodded to me.

"I've been doing some research on the figures of the size of the vein which cannot be supported by the current infrastructure..." I began.

He scoffed. "You don't think I know that?" he asked, leaning forward.

It took every ounce of control I had to remain level with my voice as I said, "Have you been in deals with railroads to expand our cargo? Have you bought the rights to the water? Have you coordinated for a new smelter plant? Have you figured out a way to stop the endless fires? How about reinforcing the current smelter plant, which is sliding down the hill day by day? Have you figured how to house these new men, much less drum up interest for their recruitment and relocation?" I felt the venom in my words, which surged with every pulsation of dull ache in my injured arm. I tried to keep the smile off my face and even lowered my head to look down at my papers as I spoke. His silence was answer enough.

"I've already done the research and found the businesses and people we need to contact for the appropriate transactions to occur. The older part of the Daisy Mine abandoned their smelter plant a few months ago and it was recently purchased for pennies. If we buy this before the new owner catches wind of the profit to be made in keeping it, we can buy it for cheap. The owner's name is Goldy Lockwood." I paused here, waiting for one of them to react. Nothing. So I surged forward. "She also owns the right to the water, which we'll need to purchase from her soon too."

"And you know how to contact this Goldy?" asked Abraham, his tone bored. Well, he attempted to sound bored, but I knew full well I had his attention. His body language always spoke volumes over his voice. He was on the edge of his seat, drumming the arm rests.

"I have her information and can act as proxy. It would be suspicious if the owners of the mine were contacting her directly, don't you think? She may catch onto the fact there's money to be made. Now, for the housing..." I laid the map flat in front of them of Jerome with various locations circled.

"These are ideal for housing because of their location and proximity to the mine. They're also close enough to the Main Street to support the businesses you both already own there." I sat back then, leaving the papers in front of them to view. "I must add a sense of urgency, given the time of year and nature of purchase. It's only a matter of time before the success of the mine goes national. And it's already December, with a January 1st open, you're far behind on smelter. If we could simply build a new smelter, I'd propose that option, but it won't be functional for months. We could always delay the opening of the mine..."

"Absolutely not," cut in Madam Jennie. I was hoping she'd agree.

"Why ever not?" asked Abraham, facing Jennie full on. "It seems it will save us a bit of cash and no haggling with some... woman I've never heard of. Who is this Goldy Lockwood?" he asked, annoyed. I rifled through my papers and handed him a newspaper article I had. This would be much easier if he'd only had a bit to drink before coming. "The daughter of a senator and investor? Looking to make her fortunes in the mines? Hmmm…" Abraham trailed off, reading through the paper once or twice more. "I should very much like to meet this Miss Lockwood once the sale is finalized."

I straightened, taking the paper from his hands. "I believe she is based out of California. I will make the needed contact this week."

"Where did you get all this information?" he asked suddenly, his eyes narrowing on me. Jennie paused as well, her hard gaze on me. I released a slow breath.

"While I was visiting family, I had a lot of time to think. I do not wish to be the manager of a brothel. I wish to have my legacy tied to the mine instead. You've both said as much. There's money to be made in the mine, more than with the brothels. I do not own land or property but this is what I am good at. I offer my services so I may be included in the pay out."

"The pay out?" he mused, sitting back in his chair as he played with the edges of his mustache.

"Yes, 22%, with an advance of $5,000 cash before the mine opens on January 1st."

"And who will pay this advance?" asked Madam Jennie. Her eyes reverted back to their normal amusement as though this were a game for her to play. She was used to being the cat, not the mouse.

"I'm sure you'll realize my offer is more than generous by the end of this meeting. After all, you have no time to find someone else to contact the owners of the smelter, property, water…" I trailed off. The two of them exchanged glances before leaning back in their chairs.

The rest of the meeting was spent discussing buying properties, dividing up incomes, and by the end of it, Abraham stayed behind to finish up talks with Madam Jennie as I headed back to the brothel to write a letter to Miss Lockwood.

The reply came a week or so later.

> *Mr. Abrahams et al.,*
>
> *I have reviewed your offer for the water rights and smelter plant at the township of Jerome, AZ and must respectfully decline your offer. When I made purchase of such properties and assets, it was after being assured of their value by my independent investigator. He sampled the contents of the mine himself and, in lieu of the ability to purchase mine rights, assured me that purchase of these assets would be the next best thing.*
>
> *I know the type of fortune you are sitting on and want to be an active part of this growth and process. I think that, combined, we can make each other very wealthy. There is enough to go around, no need to keep it amongst yourselves.*
>
> *Such as said, if your offer increases enough to make me a comfortable woman in my age, I shall relinquish my rights to both in your name. Do not seek to take advantage of a lady in her elder years.*
>
> *Yours sincerely,*
> *Goldy Lockwood*

Mr. Abraham was not thrilled.

"Her private investigator?" He practically screamed as he read the letter. At first, I thought he would tear it into pieces and throw it in the air as he was prone to do, but something like sense kept him from destroying it entirely. I was glad that my face routinely went red with embarrassment at the smallest slight, for they'd mistake its current red hue for that and not for amusement. Watching him squirm was making me happier than anticipated.

"Who is this broad? Who is this...this...uhg!" He tossed the letter into the air then and I watched the paper slowly descend onto the table. Madam Jennie looked even less amused, her arms crossed over her chest, her fingers tapping on her elbow.

"I have sent word down through the mine to alert anyone who doesn't belong and to have them removed at once. It is perhaps too little too late, but it will prevent future incidents," I offered. Jennie nodded. Abraham fumed.

"If I may," I said after a labored silence. Jennie nodded, and I took a breath. "Without water and smelter, there is no mine, and therefore, no money. Perhaps a short agreement until we can finish the building of the new smelter plant..." I pointed on the map laid out on the table to the land that was recently purchased from a Miss Angela Ruby for the purpose of building another smelter plant. That land, too, had been a bit more expensive than anticipated, but they fought through it. I had to be careful in my game. If they were bankrupted before the mine was pillaged, there'd be no wealth for me either.

"Once that is built, we can sever ties with her, or buy the water rights. She can keep the smelter, the new one will be far superior and safer." They were silent as they considered this between each other.

"She's right," Jennie said at long last, sitting upright and smoothing her skirt.

"Someone knew about the mine and now we're paying the price for the slip." Abraham laughed a malicious laugh. "Yes, you found out about the mine, and I'm paying the price for our partnership. For all we know, she told this Goldy Lockwood..."

"You're quite right. I traveled to California without any of your knowledge and made correspondence with an elderly woman, who I advised to buy a smelter and water rights to an obscure town in Arizona territory for the sole purpose of cheating you out of your money - out of our money." I let the sentence hang in the air, glad for my outburst because it sounded so ridiculous out loud he would hopefully drop the accusations. Madam Jennie laughed and shook her head.

"Abraham, you have quite the imagination. How would such a ploy benefit Louisa?" she asked, watching me closely.

I disliked the way she'd looked at me lately, a feeling I couldn't quite put a finger on. "Your wealth is my wealth," I added, taking the letter off the table and folding it neatly. "Shall I write back that you accept her terms for a partnership, at least until the mine grows more?" Abraham waved his hand dismissively and Miss Jennie sat back, silent.

I left to find Heather.

Chapter 19

IT WAS Christmas Eve when everything fell apart.

Goldy Lockwood allowed the partnership between Madam Jennie and Mr. Abraham to go through, and after allowing her to purchase a few shares of the mine ("Let the old bird have some sense of ownership," Abraham had said during one of our meetings dismissively.), they planned to go forward with the opening of the new vein. Drilling was set to begin January 2nd (they knew everyone would be too hung over on New Year's Day), Goldy sold the smelter to them for three times their original asking price, and allowed generous use of the water rights for twice the requested lien. Madam Jennie was nearly tapped out, and I was not sure how Abraham's finances would fair. I intended to find just how deep those investor's pockets were.

At first I played devil's advocate with Madam Jennie about using so much of her finances for this. What if the brothel underwent a disaster? What if anything went awry? What if the vein dried up sooner than imagined? In the end, we always came to the same point—the reward was well worth the risk.

During this time, I had a nagging sensation that something wasn't quite right with Madam Jennie. She asked for my company less and less and consulted me on zero matters through the month of December. It wasn't until Christmas Eve that she called me into her office.

"Sit," she said quietly. I did so, stiffly. She reached into her desk and pulled out a stack of papers, letters. I recognized them almost the minute I saw them.

"What are those?" I asked, trying to keep my voice steady. She leaned back in her chair.

"You tell me," she said, frowning. I reached out, slowly, to grab the letters.

Cassidy's letters.

I couldn't quite remember where I put them...did I take them with me to California? Some of them, yes. I had a sudden memory of my room being rifled through upon my return, various things misplaced. How had I missed the letters? I suppose with the knowledge I had...

"Ah," I said. I set them down in front of me, staring at them. The silence spread between the two of us longer than I thought it would. Would she speak first? Should I explain?

"As you can imagine, this is troubling for me," she said at long last. I didn't answer, still staring at the notes. Why didn't I dispose of them? Why did I keep them? Who went through my room?

"Because someone went through my things while I was gone?" I asked. She let out a short laugh, a bark really.

"Because of your affections with women, and I run a business of women."

The silence stretched longer.

Should I explain that she came onto me? "She's dead," I said at long last. Madam Jennie visibly flinched and I raised my eyes to look at her. She was wearing the same look she wore the last few weeks, watching me carefully, as though she was trying to decide something. "She was found dead in California. Murdered, they think. A robbery." I managed to keep my voice steady as I said this. What was I afraid of? My hurt? My confession?

"And how do you know this?" she asked.

I sighed. "Her cousin John told me. He sent me a letter." A lie.

"So he knew about you?" she pressed, her voice rising. I realized too late that it wasn't the right lie to tell. If I admitted to being in California, though, it was over. I should just stop talking. I should just...

"It seems this is worse than I thought. Not only are you..." she swallowed and shook her head. "But you don't even have the sense to keep quiet about it! Who knows who he'll tell?"

"And risk the reputation of his cousin and his career? Unlikely," I retorted.

She pursed her lips. "It doesn't matter, if she's dead, she has no reputation. It's easy for him, in a big place like California. Out here? If anyone knew that my business associate was a..." Again, she couldn't bring herself to say the words.

"You peddle in flesh and you worry what someone thinks of me?" I could feel tears of anger, hurt, rage rising to my eyes but I refused to let them spill over. I wouldn't let her win, not this time.

"I can't help but think you have a special interest in working here, and I cannot stand for that. I won't put these women at risk of your...lewdness. I want you gone. Now." She was firmer than I anticipated, standing imposingly across from me, her arm outstretched to the door. "After today, I never want to see your face again or hear your nonsense ideas. You're barred from this establishment. And if you so much as mention the mine, or the money, or anything, I will out you to everyone. If you care for your safety, you will be smart about your exodus."

I knew better than to argue. I stood slowly, leaving the letters on her desk, and turned to the boarding house to grab my things.

The tears threatened to fall from my face as I made my desperate dash from the brothel to the boarding house. I passed Celeste in the hallway but she didn't stop to question me. She simply gathered her jacket about her and went into the cool December air.

I burst into my room and went straight to my things, pulling them out of the armoire, completely unaware of the presence of another person in my room until I heard the unmistakable shuffle of another person.

"Ah, Miss Louisa," said Abraham. I jumped, turning to see him sitting in the chair near my bed, completely missed in my distressed entrance. He sat comfortably, lounging, a smile on his face, a pistol draped across his lap. The sight of it stopped me in my tracks.

"You look upset, has something happened?" he pressed. I swallowed, unsure if Madam Jennie told him about my dalliances. Would it be a good thing or a bad thing for him to know? I couldn't muster the brain power. "Are you packing your things to run, Louisa? Or should I call you Goldy?"

Oh.

"What are you talking about?" I finally managed, unable to tear my eyes off the pistol across his lap.

He caught my gaze and patted it, standing from the chair
and holding it in front of him, aimed at me. "Don't mind this,
it's just a tactic I use to get information I need. I'm sure you
remember how it feels to be shot, yes? Painful, really, and with
much lasting effects. I think being such close range, the bullet
will hit its intended target. I could kill you. I could maim you...
make it so you don't walk again, can't use your arm, whatever.
Permanent disfigurement would make me quite happy..." he
trailed off, waving the pistol around as he spoke. I remained
silent through this all, tracking the movements of the gun.

"You see, I did some investigating of my own. This information about some unknown woman out of California with
all this money, buying the rights to JUST the locations and
objects we need right before we utilize them. It was all too
queer, and such a cruel twist of fate. So I made some calls,
wrote some letters, and found the man who brokered the deal.
California...quite a way to travel, isn't it? But he told me all
about the red headed girl that showed up and no mention of an
elderly woman. And no record prior of a Goldy Lockwood,
except one that took a train from Jerome, Arizona to San
Diego, California the week of Thanksgiving. Didn't you head
to Kansas that very same week? I didn't take much to piece
together what you'd done.

"Except...why? Why buy all of this out from under us if
you didn't intend to screw us over somehow? Was it lashing
out because of our upcoming nuptials? I couldn't place my
finger on why, so I thought I would ask."

"Nuptials?" I asked, frowning. Abraham laughed.

"Why, yes, Madam Jennie and I are getting married. Once
the mine hits its peak and we buy the water rights back, we plan
to own Jerome, literally. It's a great match, don't you think?
The leading lady of Jerome with the leading man? We plan to

spread out, buy other mines, turn the Arizona Territory into something we control and shape. Push for statehood, create an empire. People will say nothing about the Rockefellers after we're done." He smiled broadly. "I knew it would never work out between us Louisa; you were never quite rich enough for me."

"Congratulations," I offered.

He sneered. "I have a request of you, it's quite simple really. You will hand over everything you own under whatever fake names you have, and I will let you live. Then you will leave Jerome. I will make up some story to Jennie about why you had to leave in such a hurry, and you'll never return. There will be no nonsense about this Goldy Lockwood or her associates owning things from *my* mine." His voice rose as he continued, leaning toward me. I took a step back, feeling the edges of the side table against the back of my knees. I could feel the heat from the gas lamp against my hand. So he didn't know about Jennie kicking me out. He didn't know she'd fired me just moments before. Likewise, she didn't know about my involvement in the mine.

He took a step forward, the gun just inches from my face. "Authorize the transition of all your assets to me and I'll let you live. You can find some other town to con and keep whatever petty cash you have lying around. I don't care if you die in a hole, I just want what is rightfully mine."

His finger moved to a lever on the back of the pistol, a warning of the shot he intended to take.

My hand closed around the gas lamp behind me and, with all the force I could muster, I swung it upwards to meet the side of his face. It was heavy enough to knock him out, the gas from the lamp catching and burning his face. The lamp fell to the ground next to him, fire spreading quickly across the floor.

The pine wood flooring was like tinder and before I was aware, it spread across the ground, surrounding an unconscious Abraham. In a panic, I lunged for the armoire again, this time shoving everything I could into a bag. Everything else in the room would have to stay, it wasn't important. These jewels, a few items of clothing, I threw them into my bag and raced down the hallway and out the door. I don't remember if I warned the others. I just ran.

Within twenty minutes, the entire boarding home went up in blaze. The cool winter breeze mixed with the lack of rain for weeks fed the fire until it roared. It spread to the Cathouse next door, and the businesses all along the row. Before long, the entire street was in flames. All around me people were running, bumping into me, trying to press past me to find someone to put out the fire.

But I owned the water rights they would need, and the fire department wouldn't be built until 1899.

It took hours for the blaze to run its course and take out almost the entire business district. It went from the boarding house to the brothels, down the street to the businesses and restaurants. I watched in a trance as the smoke billowed into the sky. It was a funeral pyre for all my hard work over the last year and a half. Here lay Louisa, dead and burned.

Behind me in the saloons that still stood, the bartenders were offering whiskey for free. I heard them talk amongst each other of how the fire started, as it continued to rage and destroy the strip. "I heard a woman yelling at her man," said one man to another.

"No, it started at that saloon, I watched a kerosene lamp light up the entire place." The stories continued and spiraled as the whiskey flowed readily, and I stood in the midst of the street, watching the blaze burn.

At long last, just as the sun was fading over the horizon, the fire stopped and the ash coated the sky and the air.

I made my way over the wreckage of the house. Across the way, I saw the Verde Valley, obscured by the smoke and ash. Cleopatra Hill was invisible through the haze. Mingus Mountain? I couldn't see it. Beneath me were the charred remains of the boarding house I'd lived in for half the year and next to me, the remains of the brothel I helped create.

And somewhere under the debris was Abraham, and hopefully, Madam Jennie.

Chapter 20

I DON'T KNOW how long I stood there in the wreckage when I heard a cough and turned to look behind me. Heather. She was picking through the wreckage, coughing as she called out my name.

"Heather!" I called, rushing to her.

"Oh, Louisa, I was so worried!" she said, throwing her arms around me. We embraced briefly, then she looked around quietly.

"Wow," she said to the wreckage. I nodded in agreement. "I heard about the fire and came as soon as I could, I was hoping you would be safe," she said, then narrowed her eyes at the bag I held in my hands. "How did you...oh, Louisa."

We planned to head back to Cottonwood to where she lived, but I had one last stop to make. I had one last thing to check on in Jerome before I could give up my place in it. If Madam Jennie was dead, and the evidence of my affections to Cassidy were gone, then I was safe to stay. All who wanted me dead and gone would be dead and gone themselves. At last, freedom.

We made our way through the smoky streets to ascend the hill and, finally, to my garden.

It was in shambles.

I walked slowly, soot falling off my clothing and hair in great waves, as the wind blew the wreckage of the garden across its now empty space. Every plant was pulled from the soil and uprooted, thrown to the wind, cut into pieces. The trees— someone attempted to do the same and failed. Instead, they tried to cut each branch off, or else cause other mortal injury to it. They'd succeeded in wrecking most of them, rendering their roots useless. The flowers were torn, the herbs sliced, the entire scene was more of a graveyard than anything else. I felt the tears come to my eyes now, hot and uninvited, spilling down my cheek as I watched the labor of the last nearly two years of my life destroyed.

Would the same thing happen to me if I stayed? Would this town and its ghosts and its knowledge destroy me? I couldn't take the risk. Heather placed one of her callused hands on my arm, giving a gentle squeeze. She knew better than to say anything to me in this situation and just to let me grieve. I sank to my knees and gathered a bit of basil in my hand, running my fingers over the leaves.

"We can't stay," I said at long last, looking up at Heather through my tears. She nodded knowingly.

"We knew we couldn't," she agreed. She knew long before I did that Jerome was a temporary stop for us, not a home. I nodded and stood, dusting my knees off, drying my tears.

It took two weeks to pick through all the wreckage until at long last, well into the New Year, a final body count was never really established, and the exact cause of the fire was still very much up to debate. During this time, I made an effort to not be seen, lest Madam Jennie were still alive and made good on her deal. I hid out in Cottonwood with Heather, wearing the disguise I did in California, until the final body count came in.

Mr. Abraham was listed as "unaccounted for."

I was listed as one of the dead.

Letter 1

February 2nd, 1899.

Dearest Madame Jennie and co.,

I was shocked to hear of the fire and destruction of your establishment and the desertion of our business associate, Mr. Abraham. I understand his affairs are still in the air, so I offer my condolences to you at this time of need. I understand that his will passed much of the business on to you, that makes us both wealthy women in our own rights. I hope the loss of him isn't too much for you to bear. I lost my late husband five years ago on this very day.

As for business—we must always discuss business—we should go forward with the opening of the mine. I have included correspondence with my lawyer as it appears your Miss Louisa is no longer returning my letters.

Always,

Goldy

Letter 2

February 10th, 1899.

Miss Goldy,

Thank you for your kind letter. It seems that our Miss Louisa was lost in the fire, quite a tragedy. She was a bright soul and very much an asset. Thank you for including the correspondence with your lawyer, I hope to have the estates finished and the details worked out.

It appears that I now own majority shares in the mine. Would you consider trading shares for the water rights? In light of this most recent fire, I've made an effort to establish a fire department to prevent further losses from happening. I also am not in a situation to broker with money, as the sudden loss of most of my businesses needs to be rebuilt. I've enclosed the details of the amount of shares I'm willing to trade, as well as a numerical value for the ones you can purchase right out.

The mine's opening day of January 2nd was not delayed and the vein proves to be just as plentiful as we *hoped. It's my thoughts that within the next six months, I should be able to pay for the water rights, if another catastrophe doesn't happen.*

Regards,
Madam Jennie

Letter 3

1900 - Christmas

Louisa,

I always knew you were clever, that's why I chose you to work for me. I didn't realize how clever you truly were.

It appears you are no longer a ghost that haunts the halls of the brothel, as Tabitha would have us all believe, but instead a living being that's been swindling me for years. Accept this letter as the end of our business partnership. I've wired the money to pay you off once and for all.

Never again,

Jennie

Enclosed was a clipping from a newspaper.

Chapter 21

I SHOULD KNOW by now the dangerous nature of the newspaper. It's something that can be read far and wide and sent in letters to undermine even the greatest of cons. I'd carried out my secret identity of Goldy Lockwood for over a year now, settled in the hills of northern California near San Francisco with Heather. We journeyed up there shortly after the fire and news of my death. It was the perfect opportunity to escape Jerome once and for all and start over. We had plenty of cash, and Heather had a dream to fulfill. San Francisco seemed like the perfect place.

We built an empire in that short time. Goldy Lockwood was not an elderly lady who used her late husband's fortune, she was a young redheaded woman from old money from somewhere...no one knew for sure. Just that she was young and probably fell into her fortune the way all young people did—becoming an orphan to an empire.

No one could say I wasn't self-made. When I first met with Mr. Johnson—the broker who oversaw my purchase of the smelter and various lands in Jerome, plus the water rights—I had a fair bit of cash. I did not have enough for him to be particularly impressed. I think he took pity on my melancholy and allowed me to invest in what he thought was a dead town and a dead mine. Historically, that was accurate, the mine was open once and closed down shortly after in the 1880's after it ran out of luck. It wasn't until a savvy investor reopened the mine did it flourish again, and Abraham's new vein would bring the boom that grew Jerome to a town of nearly 15,000.

But that was very much in the future.

Mr. Johnson was shocked at the price I pulled in for the smelter and the water rights, and the cost of the properties I'd bought for pennies only weeks earlier. He knew better than to question, though, as it wasn't uncommon in those days for insider trading and shady business. He took his cut and didn't ask questions.

He also helped us to buy more properties in the city and turn them into boarding facilities and housing units for the incoming population. San Francisco was booming at this time and we were just ahead of the wave. Heather and I owned 15 buildings and two restaurants by the time Christmas of 1900 rolled around. The mine proved to be the most profitable in the world and we pulled in more and more money every week.

Mr. Johnson, so shocked by the turn of fortune, insisted on a newspaper article about Goldy and her quick rise to riches. We created a story that was equal parts true and equal parts false: Goldy Lockwood was an orphan who, through good business and good sense, turned her pennies into pounds and now owned a large chunk of the west side of San Francisco. There was even a portion in the story about her younger sister, Heather, who owned an upscale boutique near the pier that turned out some of the greatest clothing in the state.

Heather went on to have a few other newspaper ads about her success, but that was not the article Jennie sent. No, Jennie sent an article showing me, stone faced, dressed like a true elite member of society, outside The Lockwood Estates. It was an upscale housing establishment I'd created from scratch. The downstairs had all the amenities a member of the upper class would expect—a bar, valets, grocer. The housing included electricity and plumbing and had rooms larger than most homes did. The rooms were fully furnished with the greatest pieces of carpentry and the finest silks any had ever seen.

The housing sold out within the first two weeks.

It was my pride and joy, and despite the stone face, I was exploding inside. It proved to be extremely profitable, and with the loss of the mine (Jennie didn't know I owned 10% in shares under various other pseudonyms that Mr. Johnson helped me to create.) would become my major breadwinner. Jennie somehow wandered upon this article and sent it, along with the letter, to my personal address.

I understood her warning but knew she could do little to back up her original threat anymore. The brothel burnt to the ground, I doubted she took those letters with her as she fled. And even if she had, at the knowledge of my death, she wouldn't have kept them, would she?

It didn't matter anyway. Louisa did not exist anymore, I was Goldy. My entire persona was changed and she had no hold on me anymore. I had more money than she did. She may have been the richest woman in the Arizona Territory, but I was the richest woman on the entire West Coast.

For some reason, though, this wasn't enough.

Why should she walk away with riches when she planned to throw me to the dust and have me killed if I ever came around again? Why should she get to live with her money, thinking I was dead and gone?

Maybe the knowledge of how I outsmarted her would be enough for me and stop the nagging sensation that she was, somehow, getting away with something.

Maybe.

Epilogue

1905 – ACME, ARIZONA TERRITORY

THE BRUNETTE WOMEN who lived at 14 West Street was notorious for her outrageous parties and sinful lifestyle. Whispers say she was (is) the richest woman in all of Arizona territory, but that man she's been with has been known for trouble. A gambling man, the type to lay up at a saloon all afternoon and wager everything including his boots and sometimes more. People have seen him around town, staggering out of a bar piss drunk, naked except for his lucky vest. His lucky vest, lucky in the sense no one would take it off his person on account of its smell.

It's not that the brunette women was a particularly attractive one. She had a spatter of spots from being out in the sun too long as a young woman and a face that was as long as the day in summer. Still, you'd think a woman with her means would have found someone better than a scrub like him. Thankfully, they had the sense not to live together, she at least kept her modesty there. She lived in a grand house just off the main drag so she could look down at the long street.

There were a lot of whispers about where she came from, something about a mine in Jerome. No one knew what happened, not really, just that she went from owning a mine and a lot of businesses up on that hill to suddenly cashing out with her lover and moving to Acme. She never spoke of it— rarely spoke to anyone, that is—and was often found sitting in the corner at her own parties, drunk within an inch of her life, hissing at people to leave.

But her parties were parties in a town with so little going on, everyone went right up until the day she died.

See, everyone has his or her theory about her death. Her lover, that gambling man who would have sold her if it were an option, shot her. Allegedly. He's going to be hanged for it next week in front of everyone in Acme and all the Arizona terri- tory. It's not that hangings are an uncommon spectacle, it's just that this brunette woman was so well-known.

But I know the truth about her death.

In 1897, she became, nearly, the sole owner of a mine after half the town of Jerome burnt down. Her business partner and (secret) fiancé was lost in the fire, presumably in a saloon. Of course his body was never found, most of the bodies were charred beyond recognition, it was assumed. The richest man in Arizona wouldn't just disappear, especially on the eve of the grand opening of his newest mine.

At first, the rebuilding of her various businesses, brothels located along the main drag of Hull Street, was a slow process. There were whispers of her immense wealth plummeting because of the fire from the previous year. She spent all her money buying up shares and water rights for the mine, she didn't have anything left over for the reconstruction of the brothels. Apparently, her new business partner, a woman out of California, had to buy a lot of her shares to give her the funds to build up the business. She rode the coat tails of the other woman, going further and further into debt, trying to rebuild her empire.

It took her two years to pay the other woman back, and by that time, the mine was so profitable that her partner was many times richer than her. At last she had the funds to regain control of the mine. That's when she met her lover, sold out her shares of the mine, and left Jerome for Acme. No one knows why she didn't stay partners with the woman, the mine was growing to be the most profitable mine in the world. The women who worked in her brothels said she'd lost a taste for the business. Then one day, seemingly out of nowhere, she came violent and angry and paranoid. Something changed, something snapped, and she left that place and everything behind her. The mine fell into the hands of a rich investor out of the east coast who continued to build the mine up. He even opened the mine as a pit to stop the fires that were burning deep in the shafts for years.

Troubles followed her. Whatever caused the rift between her and the business partner from California was enough to make her skittish. She constantly questioned her interactions with others, she didn't trust anyone she bought off of. She demanded to see the landlord in person, and never wrote letters or correspondences. She hated the invention of the telegram more than anything else. Her paranoia infiltrated her entire life, but she had enough fortune to live off that she could isolate herself appropriately. She owned the land she built her house on, which she built using her own crew. Her lover was less concerned with those details but he was too drunk most of the time to notice her paranoia. He'd just laugh it off, saying that women have their ways.

She also didn't take kindly to guests and strangers. Every new person that came through the town got a side eye from her. She was particularly hesitant around red heads. They were often kicked out of her parties in a screaming fit when she was too drunk to stand anymore. Her parties would end this way often—screaming and stomping around her house, shooing people left and right. People still came to the parties for the excellent drink and the occasional drama. Small towns loved their drama.

The night of her death didn't start off interesting. It was April, cool and calm, with the spring giving way to summer much earlier than it should have. There were no grand parties that night and the streets of Acme were relatively empty when her lover, drunk off his ass, banged on her door to get her to open it. He'd wagered a huge debt that he couldn't pay off despite all his begging and pleading, but he knew a woman that could help him. When he banged on the door, she answered, demanding to know whom he owed the debt to. He rambled on and on until she was forced to follow him down the empty street to the saloon that sat just six doors down. It was late enough at night for the saloon to be mostly empty.

He led her to a back table, where a figure sat in the shadows.

"Come out there, stranger, and let us settle this debt," she declared to the shadow. The shadow leaned forward, exposing a wildly freckled pale face and two large red eyebrows. Jennie's face turned white as her gaze traced up that large nose to the heavy head of unruly red hair, a few streaks of silver along the edges despite the younger age of the girl... Of me.

I watched the color continue to drain from her face as her eyes met my own.

"I suppose there's a debt to settle, indeed. How say you, we take this outside?" Her lover drunkenly blinked at the two. He'd have no memory of this the next day, or anything that occurred the rest of the night. The saloon wasn't crowded, but it wasn't empty either. Still, no one saw the two women and the drunken man walk outside. It wasn't uncommon for him to wander in and out of the saloon and follow whomever he wished. Sometimes complaints came back of him setting up residence in the street, or in someone's carriage, or stealing a horse and riding away. No one paid attention as he slipped into the night with the two women.

"I told you to take your money and be done with me," Madam Jennie spat at me once we were in the street.

"You also told me you'd have me killed if I ever came back to Jerome," I replied. She smirked and crossed her arms over her chest.

"I said no such thing, I just told you to leave."

"On the threat of outing me and letting everyone else kill me," I added. She didn't reply, her jaw set rigid.

"You know this girl?" her lover asked, swaying. Jennie ignored him.

"Let's get this done with, then. What do you want, Louisa?"

"Your man owes me a debt," I answered.

"I'm not paying it," she replied, her fists clenched at her side. "I told you years ago to take your money and leave me be. I sold the damn mine, I left Jerome, I hoped never to see your sorry hide again."

"You shouldn't have threatened me," I responded.

"That was years ago, are you still holding onto that?" she

hissed. "You left to California. I didn't tell anyone. I let people think you were dead, even after I figured out who you really were. I could have ousted you and made your claims to the mine illegitimate. I didn't."

I laughed. "No, but you planned to oust me from the start, before I had something you wanted. You were searching my room for some reason to get rid of me and take all the money for yourself. I know what happened to your last business partner before me, the girls would talk. You had the mine, you had the resources, all you needed was to keep it to yourself. You got lucky finding those letters, I should have burnt them in Cassidy's fireplace after I killed her."

Silence settled between us. Jennie's face changed then, shock, horror, awe...I wasn't sure. Something about the admission felt great though, like a secret I had caged in my chest for years. Telling Heather...that wasn't an admission. Heather turned out to be the greatest family I had. This was open, in the air, where anyone could hear for the first time since it happened all those years ago.

Jennie's lover sat on the ground, his head between his knees, vomiting into the dirt.

"I went to California, not Kansas, and found her that Thanksgiving. That wasn't her cousin, it was her husband. She conned us. They came and stole money from us, she told me herself. They meant to rob you but instead..." I drifted off, felling the angry tears building up in my eyes. Couldn't she see that I was protecting us? That she deserved it for lying to us, for lying to me?

"That's what it was about, don't lie. She used you and you got revenge, because you're vindictive," Jennie said, her anger more evident now than ever. She was practically screaming, stomping her foot for emphasis.

I wiped my eyes with the back of my hand. "I'm just sick of being used, it never comes around unless I have it come around. It was an accident with Cassidy and Abraham, it was an accident, but they deserved it."

"Abraham?!" She was full on screaming now.

"After you told me to leave on Christmas Eve he was waiting for me in my room with a pistol. He knew I was Goldy, he'd hired an investigator. He wanted me to sign everything over to him or else he'd maim me or kill me. I hit him with a kerosene lamp and it burnt down the entire city. You never told me you were engaged," I added.

She laughed. "Don't change the subject and put this on me. It wasn't an engagement, not really. Not truly. It was joining forces. And that excuses this? You burnt down the brothels and the entire main street? YOU?"

By now her lover was roused enough to look around, his gaze glazed over and his eyes slanted. He managed to stand, staggering in the process, grabbing anything he could to help him up. The movement was obviously too much for him as he shuddered and looked about to vomit again.

"It was an accident," I said again, feeling my chest tighten. All these years, I'd convinced myself it was an accident that I'd let the city burn like that. I could have stopped the fire at first, I knew this deep down. The kerosene took a while to catch and it could have been stopped there. Yes, the house was made of pine wood, but it could have been slowed. It could have been stopped. If I had time to grab what I did before the room was consumed, I had time to put it out. Abraham's face...that couldn't be saved. But the town? The brothel? My home?

No, not my home. Jennie made sure of that.

"It was an accident," I said for a third or fourth time, less convinced.

She laughed and crossed her arms over her chest. "You can't even convince yourself, Louisa. And here you are, traveling all the way back out to Arizona territory, for what? To finally enact your revenge for some slight from years ago? You're nothing but a petulant child, Louisa, and you always have been. Thinking the world owes you more than you got. I took you in off the street and made you something. You were planning to move on, I knew it the minute I realized how much of that money you were putting away. I helped you along when you were no longer needed. You didn't want to spend the rest of your life in that brothel, don't lie to me."

"That wasn't your decision to make! It was my decision! I should have been given more for all I did. Without me, you'd never have expanded the brothels, you wouldn't have known about the mine's possible riches, nothing. I played your game and when you didn't need me anymore, you threw me aside! Don't act like you didn't, don't for one second act like you were doing me a favor!"

Her lover swayed, pulling his pistol and leveling it at me. It was inches from my face, wavering in his drunk hand. "Don't you be yelling at my Jennie," he slurred. Why were men always pulling guns on me? "You'll forgive my debt," he added, drawing himself up tall. "Or else I'll shoot you."

Panic—it's how I always seemed to deal with these situations. I tried to duck away from the gun but he lunged with it, the pistol narrowly grazing my temple with the barrel. I wrestled with his arm to point it away from me, anywhere. In his drunkenness, he couldn't fight me off as well as he'd hoped and we both crashed to the ground, him beneath me on the ground. I tried to wrestle away from him but his grip on my arm, my bad arm, was too tight. I flailed, I kicked, I pushed the gun away from me. That's when the gun went off and he became suddenly quite still.

I staggered to my feet, feeling my body for any signs of the bullet that had dislodged. I reached down to my stomach and felt the sticky sensation of blood on my fingers, which I raised to the sky to examine under the full moon. To my surprise, I wasn't affected, the blood I felt on the front of my gown was not my own. It was his. He was on his back, blood slowly seeping from a wound in his abdomen. The gun was in my hand. How did it get in my hand?

"What have you done?" Jennie screeched, falling to her knees at his side. She was touching his head, his face, shaking him, sobbing to try to rouse him. Anything to get him to move again and stand. I watched her shoulders rise and fall in slow motion, as though everything was happening at a slower pace. Still kneeling at his side she turned to look at me, thrusting a bloody finger in my direction, "You'll hang for this, Louisa! You may have gotten away with your whore and Abraham and Jerome but not this...not this! This is where your luck runs out." Tears were streaming down her face as she turned back to him. She was rocking his nearly lifeless body now, burying her face in his own.

It was late enough at night for the street to be empty.

No one saw us.

I looked down at the gun in my hand, felt the weight of it in my palm. I thought about California and everything I had there, how Heather and I had created something amazing. How in the next few weeks, a presidential candidate was set to use my Lockwood Estate to stay in. How I was on the precipice of greatness and there was only one woman, one person, who could end this for me. If I were to be hanged in Arizona Territory for murder, Heather would lose everything she'd worked for. I couldn't escape, they'd hunt me down. Would they hang a woman? I couldn't even consider these options.

The gun felt heavy in my hands. I leveled it at Jennie and shot off a few rounds into her head, her chest, anything I could. Then I placed the gun in her lover's limp hand and ran.

The story was that he went to her to settle a bet with another member of the town; everyone came forward to claim it was them. When she refused, on account of him being a reckless drunk, he dragged her into the street and shot her multiple times before attempting to kill himself. An attempt that was unsuccessful, as the county doctor got to him in time to save his life...only for him to be hanged months later for her death.

Thank you for reading The Ashes of the Brothel! If you'd like to see more works from Katryna Lalock please head to her website at cm-deer.com/kll and sign up for her newsletter. This will give you access to new releases, bonus content for other stories and more!

About the Author

Katryna Lalock lives in the deserts of Arizona with her herd of dogs, cranky cat and loving husband. When she's not writing novels that make your toes curl she's sitting in the oppressive heat, or trying a new hobby only to discontinue it partially completed a few days later.

Lightning Source UK Ltd.
Milton Keynes UK
UKHW020633160123
415428UK00015B/716